"MAGENTA NATION"
by
Joy Scott

Copyright 2020

Published by Lightsteps Publishing

To my parents, Pearl and Lewis, my brother Rich, and my wonderful family.

"Few will have the greatness to bend history itself, but each of us can wish to change a small portion of events, and in the total, of all those acts will be written the history of this generation."

- Robert F. Kennedy

Table of Contents

Introduction

The collision was gentle — as silent and deadly as the first shark bite in "Jaws." And like that startled, doomed swimmer, we had no idea what was happening. There was just time to give each other that *"Huh?"* look, then we were somersaulting down the hill, encased in a ton of Japanese metal with wheels.

Miraculously, we landed right side up. "Get out of the car," my boyfriend yelled.

Hours later, he had departed in an ambulance, on his way to the hospital in the tiny mountain town, our destination for a relaxing day in nature. I stood at the lip of the highway, observing my poor little brown Datsun, looking like roadkill after a brontosaurus stampede. The evening desert wind had awakened, leaving me shivering slightly in my cut-off jeans and crop top. I folded my arms around my bare midriff, slightly nauseous from shock.

What now? It was long before the era of cell phones. The pocket of my cut-offs held a little money, but not much. New to this Western state, we had few friends and no family within a thousand miles. I was stranded 100 miles from my apartment and any ability to get help, pick up my boyfriend's car, and drive back up here to take care of him.

Bystanders stood around in clusters, talking about the accident, I assumed. One couple — middle-aged, grey-haired, kind of roly-poly, both wearing glasses – stole glances at me and murmured to themselves. I just sensed that the entire crowd belonged to the religious sect that was so prevalent in this area – very strict, very secretive, worshipping at elaborate temples in which God knew what happened. So foreign and somewhat frightening to my Midwestern upbringing.

The male half of the middle-aged couple walked toward me. Uh-oh. Was I going to be spirited away to some secret hideaway for conversion? Proselytized to? Told I, clearly a sinner, had gotten what was coming to me?

"You from the city?" he inquired, his eyes huge behind the bottle-thick glasses.

Well, at least he didn't say "Are you from Sodom and Gomorrah?" "Yes," I said, swallowing an unexpected lump in my throat.

"You need a ride home?"

"Yes," I responded again.

"Well, I can drive you home if you want."

I glanced at his wife, who watched me, unsmiling but not hostile. Was this safe? Well, the police had my name and number if I went missing. What choice did I have?

The ride lasted two hours, through the grayish desert without even a roadrunner or jackalope to break the monotony. Slowly it dawned on me that this man would have to make the trip back as well to the city. Rescuing me was four hours out of his day. I offered him money for gas; he refused.

Several times I thanked him for his kindness. He brushed it off. At one point he said, "My wife and I, we were just watching you, and I said to her, "I'm going to help that girl."
"I'm going to help that girl." A simple statement behind an action that made such a world of difference to me. A stranger. Clearly an outsider. But another human being in need.

I was still in such a state of shock that I completely forgot to ask him his name and get his address to write and thank them. To this day, I regret that I did not more formally acknowledge their generosity. But I've never forgotten it.

To me, this long ago, relatively minor experience is America. Kindness to strangers. Coming together in a time of crisis or need, across the divide of differences that might make us, if not enemies, then rather foreign to each other and surely members of opposite camps.

So, this is one of the reasons for this book. Because what Americans have in common is far greater and more powerful than the differences that we think separate us.

We've forgotten that truth. Let's remember it, and act on it. Let's come together about our shared vision – what is truly important. It's time for a new America. And it's up to us to create it.

"Wakanda will no longer watch from the shadows. We cannot. We must not. We will work to be an example of how we as brothers and sisters on this Earth should treat each other. Now, more than ever, the illusions of division threaten our very existence. We all know the truth: more connects us than separates us. But in times of crisis the wise build bridges, while the foolish build barriers. We must find a way to look after one another as if we were one single tribe."

– The Black Panther, "Wakanda"

Do I not destroy my enemies when I make them my friends?

— Abraham Lincoln

Chapter 1

Fractured Vision, Fractured Country

The unwanted child of divorced parents, he pulled weeds from dawn to dusk for a farmer who preached God's word on Sundays and abused the teenage helpers during the week. So, he lied about his age and ran off to join the Army.

She, a motherless orphan, washed clothes in the stream that ran by the village, her future foreordained as the caretaker of her aging father.

Then overnight, their solitary destinies changed. In the aftermath of a Great War, they met and fell in love. Together they traveled thousands of miles to America to build a life together. He found work that supported their growing family – 11 offspring in all. She devoted herself to the adored children that neither had thought they would ever have.

The siblings formed strong bonds, and then marriages, that lasted for their lifetimes. Through the next four generations, they all worked hard and flourished. Today, they remain a close-knit family.

Except for one thing: An ideological divide that is deeper and vaster than the ocean their grandparents once crossed.

From the most scarlet conservative to the bluest liberal, their beliefs about life and politics place them in direct opposition to each other, to the point where these topics are simply not discussed.

There are no villains here. Liberal or conservative, if anyone was suffering, the clan would rush to help. There would be prayers from all sides, helping hands, and understanding shoulders to cry on. They love each other.

This is my family. Maybe this is your family, too. We share the same basic values of honesty, hard work, love and respect. But how to live them – that's where the Great Divide comes in.

- Are there armed invaders and terrorists at our borders, or refugees seeking asylum?
- Is it more important to protect my hard-earned money, or share the wealth to provide a safety net for everyone?
- Should people be expected to succeed on their own, or should we level the playing field so everyone has a "fair" chance?

When beliefs clash, conflict results. Yet, behind the acrimony, there are good people who often want the same thing. If we share the same values, how can we interpret them so differently? And how can we be so mad at each other?

Pondering this question led to the writing of this book. How can good people be so polarized? Even more importantly, how can we bring ourselves together to get past these differences and work together for the common good, finding solutions to the very real problems that we face today? How can we get back in touch with the values, the beliefs, the bedrock of idealism we all share and that will power us forward as one people with a shared vision?

Who Are We Really?

Every faction defends the Declaration of Independence and the values on which America was founded. Most agree on basic religious truths from the Judeo/Christian tradition. Yet when it comes to how we organize our society and govern ourselves, we seem to be from different planets.

Historically, Americans have a tradition of being generous, optimistic, hard-working, entrepreneurial and friendly. We also have history of being bigoted, cruel to those who are different from us, self-important, self-centered, to rely on money and financial success as a gauge of self-worth, and to look down on the rest of the world.

In short, we are polarized as a nation. The individual battle between good and evil plays out in our country, just as it does everywhere else in the world and within every soul.

Yet, now the stakes are higher than at most other times. We have to find a resolution that will let us move ahead, to chart a course for survival and success in a new world.

A world that many people do not recognize is already upon us. People are upset, discontented, afraid, but as to the real cause of the turmoil, many are in the dark.

- They place blame on imaginary enemies, boogeymen invented by "leaders" who manipulate them for power and control.
- They live in information bubbles where they only hear the echoes of one set of beliefs – not truths, but beliefs.
- They place their confidence in people to uphold principles, when those individuals betray those ideals every day of their lives.
- They look down their noses and judge people who are different from them and consign them to an "other" category that makes them almost inhuman.

We are drowning in denial, argument and misinformation. Until we face the truth, however painful, we can't be victorious.

"Magenta Nation" is not a book about politics. There are no detailed recommendations about policies here. It is not a history book or an academic tome. It is a book about coming together on what is really important – finding common ground in our beliefs and our hearts.

It's about listening – and really hearing – different points of view and understanding the truth that lies under them.

It's about healing ourselves, healing each other and healing the country.

Finally, it's about vision – seeing things differently, being the change we want to see in the world, and making those changes. Once we agree on the big picture – the "what" – then we can collaborate on the "how."

With "Magenta Nation", you can make a difference. You can be the solution.

. . .

Throughout this book you will read about the idea of the "Third Force." Sometimes it takes a third force, or a new way of looking at things, to build the bridge between two opposing, entrenched ideas.

Some of these new perspectives may sound like they came out of one side of the political divide – and others will seem like they came from the other side. They are suggested because they are common sense ideas, they are a different way of looking at problems, and they can be supported by all of us because they support our common values.

The belief that we can work together is not a fantasy. Of course, conflict is inherent in our human nature. At this stage in our evolution, it's unlikely that we will all come together holding hands and singing "kumbaya." Even the Founding Fathers had bitter disputes, differing views and vocal debates. But they were united in the overarching belief in a revolutionary new idea of how people should live.

We MUST reawaken ourselves to that inspiration. Without identifying that over-arching vision, we have no common goal toward which to move. Without uniting behind a common future, we will never reach that destination.

You are invited along on this roadmap forward, starting with the individual and continuing to the rebirth of our nation. The path brings together our individual goals and responsibilities with our national goals and priorities, with practical recommendations for people, for families and communities, and for large groups responsible for leading our country.

Imagine if everyone took one step forward in that direction. What progress we would make!

So, get ready to take your step.

Exercises for Chapter 1

What is your vision for America? If our differences could be resolved, what would America look like in 10 years?

If this task seems daunting, break it down in three sections.

1. The physical – what would America look like in 10 years? Our cities, rural areas, natural preserves, oceans, skies, forests, workplaces, homes? What are we all doing to create America?

_____

_____

_____

_____

_____

_____

_____

_____

2. The mental – what attitudes do Americans have in this perfect world? What is their view of their environment, their society, their community, their families, each other, their country? What are our

beliefs about ourselves, about our country?

_____

_____

_____

_____

_____

_____

_____

3. The spiritual – what spiritual attributes are Americans committed to living in this perfect world? What is America's moral compass? It may be kindness, it may be love, it may be forgiveness, it could be any attribute or behavior that fits YOUR definition of spiritual. What values inspire us?

_____

_____

_____

_____

_____

_____

_____

_____

Pause and think about your vision of America. Hold this vision in your mind's eye. See it actually happening – the people, the cities, the environment, the farms, even the government.

Give thanks for the manifestation of this perfect America, which is being created NOW, and moment by moment.

Now, come back to the present. Do one more activity. Come up with one word that represents all that you have described and seen. It could be "cooperation." It could be "tolerance." It could be "honesty." It could be "civility." It could be "prosperity" or "security" or "ethics". Any word of your choosing that represents to yourself all that you have described. This is your IDEAL for your country. Write it down, reflect on it.

This is your personal vision for America, and you can help make it happen.

"Your beliefs become your thoughts.
Your thoughts become your words.
Your words become your actions.
Your actions become your habits.
Your habits become your values.
Your values become your destiny."

– Mahatma Gandhi

"Physical strength can never permanently withstand the impact of spiritual force."

– Franklin Delano Roosevelt

Chapter 2

The Secret Weapon for Reviving America

Getting to the new vision of America is not only about activism, communication and advocacy. We have a secret weapon at our disposal – the most powerful force of all.

You could call it "intentionality." Or the power of thought or spirit, or even prayer (and what is prayer but powerful, positive thought?). This is the powerful Third Force in co-creating our nation and our world – bridging the chasm between us.

So, if you are an atheist or a scientist and say you don't believe in this "stuff," you may want to skip this section. Then again, maybe not. Because science is proving that thoughts do have the power to influence what we call "reality" in the form of physical matter and human behavior.

Spirit is the life force – the clay of which the sculpture of our world is made. The great American mystic Edgar Cayce said, "thoughts are things," with his sources going on to explain that the spirit is the source, mind is the builder, and the physical is the result. It is up to us whether we choose to focus on good, or evil; selfishness, or selflessness; a spiritual ideal, or materialism. And to know that what we focus on, is what we are creating in our lives and in our world.

The Scientific Evidence

Let's digress for a moment and look at the growing body of scientific evidence that thoughts and intention influence our reality.

Stanford University Professor Emeritus William A. Tiller has studied the effect of thought and intentionality on matter for decades. Among other findings, his experiments demonstrated the ability to change the acid-alkaline balance (pH) in water without adding chemicals, merely by creating an intention to do so.[1]

---

[1] Dr. William A. Tiller, *The Spirit of Ma'at* Vol. 2, No. 8: "How the Power of Intention Alters Matter"

Dr. Bruce Lipton's scientific experiments in "The Biology of Belief" show that thoughts influence the growth and development of cells in our bodies.[2]

Dr. Masaru Emoto's experiments proved that thoughts could actually change the composition of water. Water exposed to various emotional stimuli – music, or words in several languages representing emotions – formed beautiful crystals, while those exposed to negative human intentions formed misshapen crystals.[3] Containers of rice subject to the same stimuli remained unspoiled longer than containers subjected to negative thoughts or ignored. Dr. Dean Radin, Ph.D., replicated Emoto's experiments with even more rigorous scientific standards, including triple-blind studies; the results were published in the "Journal of Scientific Exploration" in 2008.[4]

Other studies have found unexplained spikes in random computer-generated ones and zeros correlating with periods of global trauma. When shared emotions of fear or cohesiveness were experienced by a large number of people, these random numbers began to show patterns. A Princeton study found a huge spike in these random measurements during the attacks in New York City on September 11, 2001, attributed to "some unidentified interaction associated with human consciousness."[5]

---

[2] Dr. Bruce Lipton, "The Biology of Belief"
[3] Dr. Masaru Emoto, "The Hidden Messages in Water"
[4] Dr. Dean Radin et. al. "Effects of Distant Intention on Water Crystal Formation: A Triple-Blind Replication"
[5] Princeton University, The Global Consciousness Project, "Formal Analysis: September 11, 2001"

Another study at Princeton concluded that the impact of consciousness on electricity also supported the hypothesis that there is a consciousness "field" around us that can be changed by human thought and emotions.[6]

The implications of this research are clear: consciousness does exist, and what humans think and feel influences consciousness, including electrical and natural elements that we have previously considered to be insentient.

The Most Powerful Third Force

I'll cut to the chase and point out that the missing link in creating a better future is our spirit, our consciousness, our dedication to living by a set of spiritual ideals and by projecting these ideas into reality.

Most of you know inherently that there is more to life than what we see and feel. There is a higher power, and we have a piece of that higher power within us. We're not here on earth just to have a good time or to suffer. We're here to manifest that power in our relationships, our actions, our hearts, and our world. We are co-creators of our world.

Today, there is a growing number of Americans who describe themselves as spiritual but not religious. God may not be a part of our lives in the way that S/He and

[6]Princeton University, The Global Consciousness Project: "Multiple Field REG/RNG Recordings During a Global Event"

organized religions have been in the past. But S/He is here.

How the Founding Fathers Harnessed the Power of Spirit

After the Boston Tea Party, the colonies in the South wanted to show solidarity in democracy for their rebellious brothers up in New England, but they did not want to give the British a reason to respond with violence and recrimination. So, what did they do?

They held a prayer day. The politicians and populace of Virginia went to church to pray. The colonists came together in a way that showed their sympathy for the same cause and grew even closer as an entity. What better way is there to demonstrate the spiritual unity of the colonists and their cause? What better way is there to do so, today?

Creating That Moral Force Today

So where is this moral force today that would drive such actions? On the one hand, "service" and "saving the environment" have become almost like religions, especially among young people. They see cooperation and interconnectedness as man's natural state. They will be the ones to come together to build a new America, if we can keep it together long enough for them to get into power.

Otherwise the voices of spirituality and/or spiritual solutions of the past are diluted. Once, we had strong Christian leaders that appealed to billions. We had Nelson Mandela and Bishop Tutu who showed the world what forgiveness is. In the 1960's, Martin Luther King, Jr. inspired a nation. Television coverage of the abuse of blacks in the South roused an entire country to change racist laws – legislation passed by white men that transformed society.

Now the Catholic Church is morally and mortally wounded by its sex abuse scandals, and the Religious Right is so conservative it only speaks to its own true believers. It has become a force for isolating us, not bringing us together.

We do have the Dalai Lama, a gaggle of spiritual teachers and writers, and Oprah Winfrey to awaken us to the god within and our higher, better selves. But there is a lack, nationally and globally, of spiritual leadership, the moral force outside of a political party to consistently stand up and challenge us to be our best selves, to protest injustice and to lead us to fight it.

So, what's the answer? We, individually and collectively, must find this leadership. We must BE this leadership.

The truth is, we can never revive our country and its ideals without coming together spiritually. And it's not just through religion. It is through a unity of heart and mind and a genuine appeal, from each individual to a higher power, to help us help each other.

Those organizations that claim to be a moral force in society must find the way to collaborate and inspire us all and bring us together in our common beliefs and goals. Individuals must step up and speak out, influencing their families, neighborhoods, and communities.

Maybe someday there will be a world day of prayer for America – like the colonists held 250 years ago. Catholic, Baptist, Lutheran, Jewish, Muslim, Hindu, Presbyterian, Methodist, Church of God – all denominations, all sects, praying to revitalize this wonderful country. Or maybe it will be an entirely grassroots spiritual uprising. The power of such intention will be immense, and unstoppable.

We've Done It Before!

Think of the times Americans have come together to obtain their liberty and establish a new type of government in which people were equal and treated with fairness and justice, all of which were inspired by spiritual ideals:

- The Civil War – to abolish slavery
- The Great Depression – to overcome economic adversity and be prosperous and economically secure again
- World War II – to defeat Fascism
- The 1960's – to stop the war in Vietnam and end legal racism, and to wage war on poverty for a better future for all

All these movements were brought about by a few people consistently expressing a common intention, inspired by their spiritual beliefs.

So, imagine dozens of people expressing a positive vision for America every day, every hour, and every minute. Imagine the power of hundreds, thousands, millions harnessing this immeasurable power.

Can you say "Miracle?"

With unity of intention, this power can change our environment, our fellow Americans, our fellow humans, our world. What progress we could make! What problems we could solve!

So, let's get going.

Exercise for Chapter 2

Write down, in a couple of sentences, your prayer or intention for America. Read it daily and see it happening in your mind's eye.

_____

_____

_____

"American does not have to be cruel to be tough."

– Franklin Delano Roosevelt

Chapter 3

Why We See Things So Differently

To understand how to build bridges instead of division, we need to take a close look at how we form beliefs and how we communicate. We might describe our differences as analogous to two types of parenting described by George Lakoff's book, "Don't Think of An Elephant!"[7].

The Patriarchs

First, there is the family led by the patriarch: The strong father, the strict disciplinarian, enforcing absolute rules that guide life and decisions, and providing moral and material security. Everyone who represents "Dad" must be obeyed. Religious leaders can be Dad, government leaders can be Dad, teachers, those in authority, police, the military.

When people follow Dad's rules, law and order reigns, and God's will is done. When Dad's will is not followed, punishment must be meted out – whether it's a spanking, excommunication from church, consignment to a life of poverty, or even imprisonment.

---

[7] George Lakoff, *Don't Think of an Elephant!* pg. 18

The patriarchs' interpretation of the American values of liberty and justice is liberty to make your own way, and justice by getting your just rewards depending on how obedient and hard-working you are.

This group is more susceptible to fear – fear of loss, fear of chaos, fear of losing control over their lives. They are believers in law and order, structure, and self-sufficiency as a moral imperative. They believe,

"It's up to me to take care of myself and my family. If I can do it, everyone else ought to be able to. Why should I work hard for someone else to enjoy the fruits of my labor? If someone isn't successful, they are not working hard enough. What's good for business is good for the country and for me. After all, I'm a businessperson/working person. Economic success is essential to keep my security, the security of our country."

The Communitarians

Then, there is the family dynamic fostered by the empathetic father or mother who sees children as individuals, provides a moral framework as guidance but allows for individual differences in life choices. Children are encouraged to find their own path, with the acknowledgement that wrong choices will be made, and life will go on. There is no one way to live your life.

Their view extends beyond the family and into the community. Others outside the family should be treated with respect for their differences, and support in finding their own way in life. Life's about collaboration and compassion.

The second group has a belief system that goes something like this:

We will never be truly happy or truly good unless we help those who are less fortunate than we are. It's not enough to be successful on my own – lots of people helped me to succeed. Everyone deserves the same chances, even people different from me. We're all alike and want the same things. While some people may be doing well financially, the rest are falling behind. Protecting the wealth of the few at the detriment of the many – and of the environment – is a recipe for disaster.

Their interpretation of American values of liberty and justice is that we are entitled to the liberty to express ourselves, as long as we aren't hurting others, and to justice for everybody – including the obligation to work for that universal justice.

How We View Each Other

Each group feels the other does not understand them or respect them. Patriarchs see communitarians as looking down on them, persecuting them, wanting to destroy the institutions they believe in, arrogant, dismissive and out of touch with reality. They see them as irresponsible and stupid, unwilling to deal with reality.

Communitarians see patriarchs as unreasonable, narrow-minded, trying to subvert democracy to establish a plutocracy of the rich and to enforce their religious values on the rest of the world. They see them as the dinosaurs in the brave new world that is upon us – irresponsible and stupid, unwilling to deal with reality.

What We Unfortunately Have in Common

Lest, in reading this, you identify with one of these groups and are smugly congratulating yourself on your "rightness," think about what each group has in common. Ready for it?

It is JUDGMENT.

Whether it's categorizing people as residents of flyover states and arrogantly dismissing them as uneducated and bigoted, or deciding that half the country is egotistical, immoral and damned, we are sitting in judgment of each other. And what are we really? We are PEOPLE. We are AMERICANS. We have much more in common than we have in separation.

So just stop with the judgment. STOP IT RIGHT NOW. Put it all in an imaginary balloon and let it float out into space. It doesn't serve you and it doesn't serve us.

A Surprising Reason Why We Are Different

Back to Lakoff. He goes on to explain that these differences are due not just to what state someone lives in, or their family background and upbringing, or even their life experience.

There is a biological basis for these differing belief systems. In people who are more fearful, the amygdala – a part of the brain that controls fear – is actually larger. These people consequently feel the emotion of fear more powerfully than others. This biological inclination powers emotions and helps fuel their world view.

On the other hand, people who don't have this biological feature feel safer – safer in society, safer taking risks, safer in going in new and unfamiliar directions.

Stephen Schwartz, in his inspiring book "The 8 Laws of Change: How to be an Agent of Personal and Social Transformation," also cites this phenomenon, as well as research showing that communitarians may have "increased gray-matter volume in the anterior cingulate cortex," the region of the brain associated with courage, optimism, and the management of complexity. The research cited from the University College of London also noted that this section of the brain is smaller in patriarchs.[8]

Try this experiment: Think of people you know of who were raised in a very strict belief system and left it. Maybe they did not have the biological triggers for security that others in their patriarchal communities did. Maybe they

[8] University College London, "Left wing or right wing? It's written in the brain"

felt restricted, or questioned the judgments made on others, or somehow did not fit in with the rules governing what people should be. So, they found a more empathetic community in which to develop.

Conversely, think of people you've known who were raised in communities and families that were very accepting of differences – liberal, if you would. And the children sought out another environment entirely – a restrictive church, the military, even a cult led by a messianic, autocratic figure.

Remember the show "Family Ties"? Hippie family, conservative son? "Nurture" does not completely explain our belief systems.

So, biology is in part directing our different belief systems. That fact must be respected. These differences cannot be argued away. You can't talk someone out of their biology. A new approach is needed to find common ground.

Learning to Talk to Each Other

Lakoff's view is that we need to change the way we talk about issues, to find terminology that appeals to both groups so people will hear each other. Communication is not all cerebral – we are not half-Vulcan like "Star Trek's" Dr. Spock. Hitting someone's emotional centers with terms that are inflammatory to them is likely to derail any dialogue and opportunity for cooperation.

This is more than an exercise in finding the right terms – it's speaking in terms that reflect common values.

And what are our common values? Yes, we do have them. They exist in my family. They would be espoused by those with differing views around the Thanksgiving dinner table. And they are subscribed to by patriarchs and communitarians alike. What are they?

- We love our families.
- We love our country.
- We want to live meaningful lives.
- We are inherently kind, generous and fair.
- We are pragmatic – this is Planet Earth and solutions must work in the real world.
- We believe that by acting together, we can overcome obstacles.
- We believe in liberty and justice for all.
- We are souls, seeking our true selves and something more meaningful than our physical existence.
- We share ideas of humanitarianism and morality that we want to see in our lives and in our country.

So, how to bridge the divide?

The Third Force in Communication

Here's where the idea of the "Third Force" comes in. Arguments can go back and forth, back and forth, like a tennis ball being lobbed over a net. It goes on forever.

There is no end. UNLESS along comes a completely different option – a new idea, a brainstorm – the Third Force. The Third Force is a major theme and solution in this book. Let's apply it to one area – language.

Here's a lexicon of divisive terms that are deeply believed by each group, and terms that can replace them because they reflect our common values.

Patriarchs	Communitarians	The Third Force Bridge
Law and order	Oppression and Fascism	Safety
Capitalism	Tyranny of the wealthy	Opportunity, productivity, economic prosperity
Handouts and welfare	The social safety net	Investing in all our people/Protecting our human capital
Save the wealth for us today and tomorrow	Share the wealth	Invest in America, for today and tomorrow
Taxes and big government	The social safety net	Invest in our society and in developing shared resources
The free market of health care	Medicare for all	A healthy America
Protection from immigrants who may be terrorists, and who sap our economy	Give everyone a chance	A safe and fair immigration system with obligations on immigrants
Pay for your college	Free college	Invest in affordable education with obligations on the students who receive it

Less government	Big government	Responsible, accountable government
Losing my rights	Affirmative action	A fair deal for everybody
Giving in	Compromise	A new type of leadership
Be practical	Be generous	Be fair
Losing my power	Sacrificing my principles	Finding the right solutions for everyone
Losing America	Betraying America	Find the true America of our dreams
Individual freedom	Individual justice	Individual responsibility
Republican	Democrat	American

OK, let's get real. There are people on the fringes of these belief systems who will never change, and this book won't fix that. But there are enough people in the middle, maybe leaning one way or the other, people who can take a step closer to those they perceive as being on the other side, and come together to find a way to move forward. Let's not call them the moral majority, or the silent majority, but the new leaders – those who want a future for our country and our people and know that we have to work to get there.

Exercises for Chapter 3

1. Are you part of a patriarchal belief system, or a communitarian belief system? How do you know?

_____

_____

_____

_____

2. If you were to speak to someone in the belief system that you <u>don't</u> belong to, what commitment would you make to them if it could heal America?

_____

_____

_____

_____

_____

3. If you were to give up something of your own belief system, or compromise to reach an agreement to move this country forward, what would it be?

_____

_____

_____

_____

_____

4. Go back to your ideal for America from Chapter 1. Do you have beliefs that might be preventing America from realizing that ideal? What are they? Would you be willing to change them?

_____

_____

_____

_____

_____

"And so, my fellow Americans: ask not what your country can do for you – ask what you can do for your country. My fellow citizens of the world: ask not what America can do

for you, but what together we can do for the freedom of man."

— President John F. Kennedy

Man's seeking to be helpful to his fellow man... these principles were inculcated into the Declaration... of Freedom..."

— Edgar Cayce (5023-2)

Chapter 4

The Elephant in America's Kitchen

The stink of cigarette smoke, clink of ice in glasses, the bitter taste of those drinks that grown-ups liked. It was a cocktail party at my house, and the 8-year-old me was hanging around the fringe, in my persistent quest to understand these strange beings known as "adults".

A new family had just moved in and our community was meeting them for the first time. The men all wore dark suits, and the women, "cocktail" dresses which seemed to be mostly black and white and require pearl necklaces.

Our new neighbor did something in business called "real estate."

"Yup," he intoned. "Last year was a great year. And we worked it out so that we didn't even have to pay any taxes!"

He looked to my father for a response. And Dad, who was always polite, did something very odd. He said nothing.

The new guy tried again. "In fact, we've been so smart with our taxes, we haven't paid anything for the last three years!"

He waited for approbation. And still, my father said nothing.

Later, I asked Dad what was going on. Why he was so quiet? I knew what taxes were – something you paid the government. So, what exactly were they talking about?

"It's not right," he told me. "We should all pay some taxes. We all benefit from what the taxes pay for. Like the roads. The trash collection. The post office. The Army. We should all be paying our fair share for those things."

This was a revelation to me. Dad was a successful businessman himself. He was a veteran – a prisoner of war in World War II who had come very close to paying the ultimate price for our freedom when his plane was shot down. And he thought that we were all obligated to pay our fair share to live in America. Failing to do so was dishonorable, and shameful. It's a lesson I absorbed then and have never forgotten.

Success in America is often viewed as the amount of money accumulated by an individual. It's a tribute to good old American know-how and discipline. A belief that hard work spells success is part of our DNA.

Indeed, Americans are pioneers and entrepreneurs, always looking for a new and better way. From the first immigrants to reach our shores (even the Native Americans) we were looking for a better life – freedom to practice religion, escape from poverty, more mammoth to hunt.[9]

And the way to that better life? Self-sufficiency. Hard work. Inventiveness. Intelligence. Persistence.

Yes, those are our values. We all believe in them.

The Truth About Living These Values

Now, I'm going to say something that may sound heretical.

Many of those who most espouse these values are betraying them.

No, it's not about political division. It's about <u>entitlement</u>.

---

[9] The exception, of course, are the slaves brought here from Africa against their will. They certainly weren't looking for a better life. And we're still suffering from the collective karma of those actions.

Entitlement is a disease that is sapping our moral core. Whereas once everyone was expected to contribute, now it seems like many Americans believe they should have a free ride, by virtue of their nationality, their heritage, their ancestors, or their wealth. They believe they have the freedom to do anything, and never pay the price.

Too many see "responsibility" and "patriotism" as something for the other guy. Too many are complacent and feel like they – or their ancestors – did their part and now they are just entitled to reap the benefits, even if it's the result of someone else's labor. It's in extreme form, the attitude manifests itself as dishonest behavior, gaming the system, and cheating others – all because it's a "right" to do so.

And if you're thinking "entitled spoiled kids," you are wrong. Much has been written about the trophy generation – the kids who got trophies for showing up – and how it has sapped their ambition and drive to make it on their own.

Well, young people are the ones who "get it." They understand that our future depends on us working not to compete against each other, but to collaborate. They support one another. They have high ethical standards. They believe in fairness. They have adopted service as a way of life. They are leading the grassroots advocacy to preserve a future for America.

The True Entitled

No, it's more likely the middle-aged and up crowd who are today's entitled brats. I'm ashamed to admit that it's often my own generation, the ones who fought for justice in the 60's and lost their ideals somewhere along the way as we acquired bank accounts, business suits and dependents.

The desire to protect one's own is paramount in our species. BUT – what about the tribe? Isn't the tribe more than the people at the country club?

Yes, there are people who may use circumstances of birth, race, or bad luck to believe they are now entitled to be taken care of should be given preferential treatment. But by and large, the entitled are the wealthy, who want to get richer, and the people who think it doesn't matter what they do politically and economically – someone else will take care of it.

Well, SNAP OUT OF IT.

NO ONE GETS A FREE RIDE IN AMERICA. NO ONE. <u>You live in America, you owe America.</u>

Our ancestors, up to the Silent Generation that fought World War II, understood this obligation. They also understood the concept of "service" as a responsibility, and a way for personal salvation. Going back again to the great mystic Edgar Cayce, his messages consistently stressed the importance of service in realizing our true divine nature and completing our obligations on planet earth. It's the cure for self-pity – help someone else. It is a requirement to personal satisfaction in life – selfishness does not lead to happiness.

Think about the many ways in which Americans don't step up and fulfill their responsibilities as citizens of this wonderful country, and in the many ways we miss opportunities to serve.

Financial

- Cheating on taxes.
- Cheating in business to pay less taxes.
- Taking aid from the government when you could be self-sufficient (this ranges from food stamps to unemployment to subsidies you really don't need). And yes, this aid should be available to people who need it. No one in America should be hungry, unemployed or homeless. But sometimes, people take the money when they really don't need it.
- Bending or violating business laws or business ethics for profit.
- Overspending and declaring bankruptcy to avoid responsibility for your actions.

Civic Responsibility

- Failing to vote. The U.S. has one of the lowest voter turnouts of the developed countries. In contrast, some nations fine people who don't vote.

- ❓ Voting only for people who will act to benefit you, versus benefiting the entire country overall.
- ❓ Failing to understand our government, the issues and the leaders. This lack of understanding can in part be laid at the feet of our educational system. Everyone has the responsibility to understand what's going on in America.
- ❓ Staying in a "bubble", only reading or listening to media that agrees with you, and being with people who are like you. We are a diverse society and need to face up to that fact. The echo chamber blinds us to reality.

Social Justice

- ❓ Selling out the values of liberty and justice for all by excluding certain groups.
- ❓ Being willing to sacrifice the environment and this planet's resources that future generations will need, for short-term financial gain.
- ❓ Failing to support causes that help people in need – either by not volunteering for anything, or not contributing financially.
- ❓ Failing to take care of your property so that others are safe.
- ❓ Failing to reach out to a child or family you know is having problems.
- ❓ Failing to stand up and act on what you believe in the face of injustice.

Self-responsibility

- ☐ Skating through your job or school or other responsibilities without really giving it your best.
- ☐ Abusing your health so that you're likely to get ill. Even if you think "insurance covers it," the fact is that lifestyle-related illnesses cost everybody.
- ☐ Driving recklessly, or under the influence of alcohol or drugs.
- ☐ Emotionally or physically abusing children, or knowing of these situations and doing nothing. The children growing up in adverse circumstances have a very hard time becoming successful adults, and they often become a drain on "the system." The cycle continues when they grow up and have their own families. To secure our future we need to take responsibility with a new tolerance for damaging children.
- ☐ Impairing your ability to function as a responsible, self-supporting adult by abusing alcohol or drugs.

Whew! If you've never done any of these things, step over here and receive your halo.

Yes, we are all guilty of failing to live up to our responsibilities to our country and our fellow man. Time to stop pointing fingers out there and look inside ourselves. Don't feel guilty – just recognize your situation or attitude, and change.

Warning: "Magenta Nation's" look at building the American dream contains some rather controversial and revolutionary recommendations that spread the responsibility for action and accountability evenly, even to some people and in some ways that may sound heretical. There are no sacred cows. Brace yourselves and keep an open mind.

And add this to our list of values we hold in common: <u>Everyone living in America, owes America. No one gets a free ride.</u>

Exercises for Chapter 4

1. Make a list of any ways in which you are giving back to your country and your fellow citizens.

_____

_____

_____

_____

_____

2. Make a list of opportunities you are missing. What are you doing/can you do to change that? Keep in mind that what you change may be your attitude.

_____

_____

_____

_____

_____

"The problems of the world cannot possibly be solved by skeptics or cynics whose horizons are limited by the obvious realities. We need men who can dream of things that never were... and ask why not."

— John F. Kennedy

Chapter 5

Times Are A-Changing – and So Must We

Our gift of freedom was won and defended by our ancestors and by our fighting forces today in hard-fought combat. My ancestors were part of the battle. I treasure and honor their sacrifices.

A mystical and sacred awakening occurred in 1776, leaving us a precious gift. The idea of equality among men had never before been used as a theory of government or a code of ethics. Always it had been the privileged classes, and then everyone else. One's fate was determined by the accident of one's birth. No more.

But to be honest, in the beginning it was still all about the privileged classes - wealthy, land-owning white men. Over time, wisdom and our own spiritual and intellectual evolution extended that privilege and responsibility to women and other races.

We laud these early patriots and their achievements. And we should never give up on their ideal of a society based on equality and liberty.

But the fact is, the world has changed. Then, an individual could go off into the woods and make a home and living – provided he was not killed by wild beasts or human enemies, or succumbed to privation or disease. Is that level of self-sufficiency and independence available today?

Well, maybe to a few hardy survivalists. But for the rest of us, not really. The air we breathe, the information we receive, the houses we live in, the way we earn our living, the health we enjoy, the food we eat – all are influenced by other people and a complex, interwoven, matrixed society that is like the skein of a trillion spiders' webs.

What we do affects others in ways that were impossible to foresee 250 years ago. If members of our community are sick, hungry, destructive, and hopeless, it affects all of us in ways our forefathers could not have imagined. We are so interrelated we can't really pull ourselves apart into the independent silos of old.

We must redefine freedom in today's terms.

The idea of looking at our freedoms in a new way is frightening. It may sound heretical, but it's time. We cannot lose what we have fought so long for and cherished. Instead, we must define freedom to fit the realities of life today. And what criteria should be used?

1. Liberty and justice for all. If someone exercises his or her freedom in a way that harms others, that freedom must be curtailed.

2. The Golden Rule. Do unto others as you would have them do unto you. Because of our interconnectedness, we

have to re-evaluate what actually causes harm to others and be responsible for our actions.

3. <u>Common sense</u>. Our resources – at least from our current perspective – are finite. Our problems are prolific. Our decisions are life-changing – and hopefully, life-sustaining. Protecting someone's "freedom" to act in ways that destroy our economy, our environment, or our ability to be safe from attack can't be tolerated. We need to get down off the soapbox and use our brains and common sense to define new boundaries.

4. <u>Accountability</u>. Down with entitlement – the smug arrogance that "it's all about me." We are all our brothers' keepers.

5. <u>Protecting truth.</u> Lying (via online sources, social media, or the news media) should not be tolerated. American and foreign propaganda is brainwashing our citizens. It needs to stop.

If It's Working for Me, Why Bother?

Many would say, *"if we are doing well and happy with the status quo, why change it?"* Indeed, some are doing very well.

The answer to why we have to change is this: Forces are at work that are going to change it anyway, so we may as well take control.

Right now, we are like the first seasons of "Game of Thrones." It's all about scheming for power, killing the good guys who are too honorable to kill the bad guys first, believing our great big dragons will protect us or our rich powerful family will save us, and ignoring those crazies who rant about the frozen zombies coming south to do us in.

It's time to wake up and get the message: This petty infighting does not matter. The White Walkers are coming. They will be here. They will destroy us. Our only chance is to put aside our differences, band together NOW and take a united stand.

Consider these imminent dangers:

1. Climate change is threatening us. Rising temperatures and changes in weather and precipitation are doing more than causing destructive storms. They are preventing people from growing the food they need to survive.[10]

   The immigrants to the U.S. that are such a cause of divisiveness and fear are not terrorists trying to break into the country to destroy us. Many of them are refugees, in large part affected by climate change. Look around the globe – terrorism is driven in large part by changes in our planet that are

---

[10]Soil Science Society of America, "How will Climate Change Affect Agriculture?"

causing drought and affecting the food supply[11]. Pretending otherwise is denying reality.

2. <u>Wealth distribution is punishing us.</u> The resources of our planet are increasingly concentrated in the hands of a few uber-wealthy individuals and groups. The rest of us are working harder every day for less.

    A well-orchestrated campaign to convince people that tax cuts (which benefit the rich) and trickle-down economics (which benefit the rich) are good for the average American has convinced generations that by supporting these practices, they are supporting free enterprise – a capitalistic system in which everyone can grow up and be a tycoon.

    The reality is that rich people grow richer and everyone else loses. It is impossible today for average Americans to earn enough to fund their retirement, send their children to college, take care of aging parents and pay for their family's health care. Impossible.

3. <u>Global conflict threatens us.</u> Two oceans on either side will not protect us. And the wealth gap is behind much of the unrest we see in the world today. While this conflict may mask itself as religious wars and power struggles, the underlying cause is poverty.

---

[11] Justin Worland, *TIME*: "Why Climate Change and Terrorism are Connected"

Watching a world on television where a small percent of the people in the world live in unparalleled security and luxury, and the rest shiver with cold and resentment outside the zones of affluence will never create world peace. No wall is big enough or high enough to protect the "haves" from the "have-nots."

4. <u>The rise of smart machines is changing the world of work.</u> A generation ago, the Rust Belt was born when manufacturing began to move to countries with cheaper labor and better production systems. Millions lost jobs that had been secure for generations. As a country, free enterprise thinking ruled – people who were suddenly unemployed should just go out and find another job.

Well, that's not feasible when this kind of massive dislocation occurs. We still suffer from that situation today – in the form of people who slipped from middle class to poverty and can't get out, sliding into despair, drug addiction, broken families, and a cynicism about this country and the people in it who don't care about them.

We are about to have another economic transformation that will make the 1980's look like a cake walk. As machines become smarter, the workplace and jobs as we know it are going to be transformed. How are we as a society preparing for this massive change? "Every man for himself" is not the solution. We need a plan, as a nation and as a society.

If this list of major problems has depressed you, well, it should make us all stop and think. If you think only a miracle can save us, you may be right. However, it has happened before.

We Can – and Have – Worked Miracles

In 1989, the miracle was the sudden, out-of-the-blue collapse of communism, symbolized by the destruction of the Berlin Wall. Those of us growing up during the Cold War could not believe it. Raised to hide under our desks during imaginary air raid drills, watch newsreels of underground shelters and mushroom clouds, live in fear of "The Bomb," it was simply not possible that suddenly, what we had feared and despised was – well, just over.

Here's another miracle. A small band of rebels took on the mightiest nation on earth ... and won. These educated and often wealthy landowner leaders, and the farmers, carpenters, blacksmiths, and shopkeepers, risked their lives and their families and a grisly death as traitors if they failed, because they believed in an ideal.

Imagine George Washington and his forces at Valley Forge – broke, hungry, freezing, shoeless. Did they give up? No. They staged an unimaginably daring raid in the dead of winter and captured the enemy camp across the river. The colonists were back in the game.

These are times requiring daring, imagination, courage, ingenuity and, above all, faith.

And, if you still think it can't be done, consider this.

Every mass movement in the world starts with an idea. Thoreau in his hut at Walden Pond, contemplating the nature of man and his responsibility to others and to the world. Mahatma Gandhi absorbing Thoreau's ideas of non-violence and freeing a nation. Martin Luther King, Jr. adopting those same precepts and freeing a people.

Look at the world's major movements and how they started. A carpenter in a conquered nation established Christianity. A discontented priest named Martin Luther launched a revival of religion and a new movement. A tiny religious sect – the Quakers – brought about major American reform, from abolition to women's suffrage to protecting the environment. "Truths" and absolutes about our world can be changed in a lifetime. It can happen in ours.

Exercises for Chapter 5

Go back to your ideal vision of America. Look at each of the four challenges described above. Take each one and describe how your ideal for America could be applied to resolve it. Let your imagination run wild.

1. Climate change.

_____

_____

_____

_____

_____

_____

2. Changing the distribution of wealth.

_____

_____

_____

_____

_____

_____

3. Global conflict.

_____

_____

_____

_____

_____

_____

4. The artificial intelligence revolution.

_____

_____

_____

_____

_____

_____

"The purpose of life is to contribute in some way to making things better."

– Robert F. Kennedy

Chapter 6

An Honest Look in the Mirror at Our Country

If we're going to deal with our problems realistically, we have to look at ourselves just as realistically. We have to be brave enough to take a good look in the mirror and deal not just with what we want to see, or used to see, but what really is.

Take a look at some myths we hold that can stand in the way of our progress today.

Myth # 1

If we just keep to ourselves and focus on us, we can save ourselves.

Quick – name all the civilizations that built a wall and kept themselves safe for eternity.

Well?

The magnificent Roman Empire fell to barbarians. The Berlin Wall collapsed under the weight of the people's passion for freedom and the sheer cost of keeping them controlled. The Great Wall of China lasted 5,000 years – but today it wouldn't last five days with military weapons, drones, and other modern technology.

Isolationism is no longer a solution.

Myth # 2

The old ways are the best ways.

Let's keep doing the same-old-same-old and eventually, things will settle down. Really? Can we go back to a rural agrarian society, with the average person barely literate, no antibiotics and marauding invaders an everyday danger? Maybe if there's a global cataclysm. But as a choice for changing our future? Not desirable.

Myth # 3

It doesn't affect me. I'm OK and I'll stay OK.

See Myth #1.

Myth # 4

It's all a conspiracy theory. Things are really fine.

Many people believe that there is some vast conspiracy – aliens, dark government, global conglomerates, Silicon Valley, the list goes on – that is behind the scenes pulling the strings that manage the façade we think is reality.

On one hand, government entities in the shadows are able to follow billions of people and control them. On the other, these same bumbling bureaucrats can't efficiently manage the process of giving you a driver's license.

Well, which is it?

The reality is that what we see are humans acting like humans – grasping for power, trying to take care of their families, hurting others out of fear. It has been the same for tens of thousands of years.

With one exception...

When Julius Caesar was a young man, he was captured and held for ransom by pirates. During his captivity, he had a great time – drinking and carousing with his pirate buddies. Eventually the ransom was paid, and Julius went home. Several years later, he returned with his Roman legions. Ten thousand pirates were captured and crucified – a slow, agonizing death for his former "friends."

And no one thought anything of it.

If someone did that today, what would happen? It would be all over the Internet in a second and the world would be outraged.

The point is that the cruel, inhuman treatment that our species accepted for millennia is now considered an outrage. The compassion meter has gone up. As a species, we have evolved.

Atrocities still happen. But for the most part, they aren't condoned. They are protested. The perpetrators are condemned. The victims have sympathy and compassion. We _are_ evolving – emotionally, mentally and spiritually.

And we will keep evolving.

Myth # 5

We can figure this out.

Certainly, we have the brain power to solve problems. We have ideas. We don't lack in creativity. The people who built the tower of Babel were smart, too. But they couldn't agree – and it drove them to failure and divisiveness.

The fact is humans are more than mental gymnasts. We are emotional, feeling beings as well as brainiacs. And our emotions get in the way of our collaboration.

Our egos get bruised. We hold grudges. We get fearful and resort to power games. We want to be right so badly we look to an invisible higher authority that speaks only to us, and demand that everyone else obey us. All kinds of things get in the way. In short, human nature intervenes.

How do we overcome our individual and collective frailties? Is it by finding the heroes and blindly following them? Leaders are wonderful, and they are needed.

But that's not what America was built on. It was built on thinking for yourself and respecting and acting on your own beliefs. And then cooperating to reach solid, mutually acceptable decisions.

Myth # 6

This problem is just too big for me. I can't solve it, can't make a difference and can't fix it. I'll just go about my business and hope other people can figure it out.

The fact that you are reading this says you do care. If you sometimes feel hopeless, join the club. Everyone does. But that doesn't mean you stop trying. Our individual actions and thoughts add up to collective impact.

Imagine life as a scale, held by the blind Goddess of Justice. Every good action is a grain of sand on the "good side" of the scale. Every bad action goes on the other side. Our goal is to collectively outbalance the bad with the good.

In the 2016 election, a candidate became president not because the majority of the American people wanted him, but because of flaws in the election process, millions of dollars of Russian propaganda, and many people not voting. Frequently, elections are decided by only a few votes that separate winners and losers. Yes, every vote counts. Yes, every grain of sand on the scale of justice counts. Yes, what you do matters.

Exercises for Chapter 6

We are all natural judges and critics. We all get frustrated with people who stand in the way of what we think is important.

However, unless we recognize the value in what others believe and do, we are trapped in judgment and that doesn't get us anywhere. We need to move away from our own intolerance (without of course sacrificing our own values) and find some common ground. It starts with seeing and acknowledging the other person's point of view.

1. Write down your thoughts that are critical or judgmental about people who believe differently than you about America. Start with: *I can't stand (situation or action). I can't stand it when people (action). I'm really afraid that (situation) is going to happen in America.*

_____

_____

_____

_____

_____

_____

_____

2. Now, go back and reframe every fear or criticism as a positive statement affirming an ideal or good characteristic.

    For example:

    I can't stand it that people use "religion" to justify beliefs that violate the freedom of others. I'm afraid of losing my freedom to act according to my own values.
    To:
    I appreciate the religious devotion of Americans and see those beliefs shaping a more compassionate America.

    I can't stand it that do-gooders want to take our nation's wealth and give it away to people who are not deserving. I'm afraid we'll all end up broke.
    To:
    I appreciate that the generous spirit of America can find solutions that will preserve a strong economy and provide economic opportunity and justice for all of us.

    _____

    _____

    _____

    _____

    _____

_____

_____

_____

3. When these negative thoughts or comments come up for you, practice replacing them with your positive perspective. <u>This is a vital part of setting intentions. Every positive thought you put out, moves us further along the path to unity.</u> Negative thoughts move us AWAY from our goals.

"The only thing we have to fear, is fear itself."

— President Franklin D. Roosevelt

Chapter 7

Facing Our Fears

When vagrants and hobos came 'round the back door, Grandma fed them whatever she could scrounge up. She knew they were good people who simply could not find jobs. My uncles were themselves "riding the rails" looking for work. The flames of revolution were burning again among people desperate enough to topple the government to find an answer, any answer, to stop the suffering.

The Great Depression was perhaps the lowest point in American history. One out of four workers were jobless. Even the wealthy, whose greed fueled the stock market crash, were struggling.

And who led America out of that trough of despair? The President who intoned, "The only thing we have to fear is fear itself." An unflappable optimist who inspired the hopeless to carry on, because there was a way out of their misery. Who himself was handicapped and physically limited, but who had the inspiration and the will to move forward and serve his nation.

The Danger of Fear

Fear is the enemy to renewing America and finding our center, our heart, again. Ironically, after coming to the brink of disaster with the Great Recession, the American economy is more robust than it has been in decades. Yet some continue to fear for their wealth. They are driven to acquire more, more, more in a quest for security and ego gratification.

The truth about fear is: we can't escape it. Really. It's been said that "no one gets away with a perfect life." It is the nature of the human condition that there is loss, disappointment, betrayal, sickness, death, danger.

You could say that it started in the Garden of Eden with the first sin. Our human nature and our destiny are such that we are mortal, and will experience the trappings of mortality no matter how much we try to protect ourselves and our loved ones.

There was a best-selling book a while back called "When Bad Things Happen to Good People[12]." I read it with some skepticism, and at the same time with a passionate hope that maybe this book had some answers to the injustices that plagued me and challenged my faith.

So, after wading through all the possible reasons for tragedy in our lives – from secret sin to reincarnation to an indifferent God to the devil – I came to the end of the book. Bad things happen to good people because – they just do. It is the reality of the human life we live. We can take precautions, but there is nothing we can do to assure that we can escape loss and pain.

The danger of having too much fear is that it leaves us open to manipulation. If we are fearful of people different from us, a powerful figure can convince us that those people are out to hurt us – or our way of life – and we have to mobilize to defend ourselves against them. If we are fearful of the unknown, we can be convinced that there are secret conspiracies against us, and we have to

---

[12] Harold Kushner, "When Bad Things Happen to Good People"

fight them. If we are fearful of sin, religious leaders can use that fear to control our behavior.

The Fear Antidote

The dangers we face are as old as mankind. And they have been real. Dangers are still real, but in many ways we don't recognize what they really are and so we don't take the right steps to protect ourselves. We are fighting bogeymen while the real monsters are winning.

So, what's the solution? We need to accept that fear and danger are a part of our lives. We have to take a solid, rational look at what is really going on in our world and agree on the most important causes to get behind. And we need to get behind them TOGETHER. If we act as our brother's keepers, we have protection. Not complete safety, but help and a buffer against the vagaries of fate. It is in cooperation and common belief that we can protect each other.

Exercises for Chapter 7

1. What are your greatest fears?

_____

_____

_____

_____

_____

2. How do you protect yourself against these fears?

_____

_____

_____

_____

_____

_____

3. Will your methods of protection work to protect you?
Why or why not?

_____

_____

_____

_____

_____

4. How could cooperation or help from others help protect you from these fears?

_____

_____

_____

_____

_____

_____

5. What could change in America that could help you be less fearful?

_____

_____

_____

_____

_____

_____

Section II

Coming Together on What Divides Us

"Each time a man stands up for an ideal, or acts to improve the lot of others, or strikes out against injustice, he sends forth a tiny ripple of hope, and crossing each other from a million different centers of energy and daring, those ripples build a current that can sweep down the mightiest walls of oppression and resistance."

– Robert F. Kennedy

The Third Force in Action – Mind is the Builder

Now let's dive into some Third Force ideas about common issues that separate us. The following chapters look at these issues, the facts about them, opposing views, the Third Force concepts that bridge the gaps, and the obligation that Americans have in this area.

Again, although policies are required to solve many of these issues, "Magenta Nation" is not about policies. It is about the principles on which we can degree to move forward. Some of them may be startling, but they make sense and are aligned the general values we all share.

As you read this section, think about your own ideas for solutions and write them down! Yours may be the undiscovered, most powerful Third Force idea yet!

Chapter 8

Climate Change and the Environment: Saving Our Future

Some said it's a school day, and kids ought to be in class like usual. But the students said "No". "Usual" doesn't matter anymore. "Regular" life is no longer an option. Life as we know it is under siege – and they are taking action.

March 15, 2019 marked the first global walk-out by students to demand action on climate change. Inspired by a young girl in Sweden, teens and even pre-teens organized Friday walkouts at their schools because the failure of adults to act on climate change was threatening their future – not just changing it, but negating their chance to have a future.

These young people see what's happening, and they are calling BS on the so-called grown-ups who are failing to live up to their responsibilities. They are becoming the Third Force for dealing with this dangerous reality that is shaping their lives.

History Repeating Itself

Why aren't adults acting responsibly? There is a parallel between their inaction today and events 100 years ago.

The greatest economic depression in the world, and our present threat posed by climate change have the same origin story – greed.

Rising stock prices fueled a rush to invest in the stock market in the 1920s, with people putting more of their disposable income and even mortgaging houses to be able to buy more stocks.

By 1929, millions of shares were carried on margin, meaning their purchase was financed with loans to be repaid with profits from the increasing values of stock.

Declining prices in October 1929 created a panic, and people rushed to liquidate their stocks, further exacerbating the losses.[13] The solution to the problem required a massive effort from citizens and from government, in the form of the famous New Deal.

We now find ourselves in a similar world-threatening situation, one caused by natural forces, human behavior and greed, for which the fix may be a new take on the classic New Deal.

For decades, major corporations and smaller businesses alike have profited through business investments and enterprises that created pollution and damaged the environment.

Consistently, these large businesses and the wealthy investors behind them have misled the public about the true nature of climate change and the risks of fossil fuels. For example, two Harvard researchers analyzed research published by Exxon from 1977-2014, and found that while the research was in line with current scientific thinking, 80% of their statements to the public (which are often viewed much more often) were doubtful of climate change.[14]

Why Deny Reality?

It's not surprising that companies fight against regulatory efforts to combat climate change. These regulations are seen as a threat to their profitability. What is surprising is

---

[13] *Encyclopedia Britannica*: "Causes of the Great Depression"

[14] John Schwartz, *The New York Times*, "Exxon Misled the Public on Climate Change, Study Says"

the success of this misinformation in deceiving the public and even lawmakers that climate change is not real.

We now have a polarization that is stymying action needed to achieve real solutions.

The Positions

In the patriarchal group, some flatly deny that climate change exists, and these people often point to cold weather to refute global warming. Another objection is that climate change science is propagated by liberals who manipulate data. Others say that climate change is happening but can't be caused by humans, sometimes for religious reasons.

They resist action because they say it will mean economic/monetary loss for people – very often themselves.

The communitarians believe that not only is climate change happening, but it is being accelerated by human activity. They see climate change as an urgent threat and a high priority, and advocate for green energy policies that preserve resources, embrace alternative energies, and protect nature.

Relevant Facts

- ⬚ The Arctic ice cap has melted, and ships can now conduct cruises on the Arctic Sea.

- The target temperature level increase for the international community has been set at 1.5 degrees Celsius as an achievable goal and a result that would stave off the most calamitous effects, according to the Intergovernmental Panel on Climate Change. (IPCC)
- The IPCC concluded that "rapid, far-reaching, and unprecedented action" is required to achieve this target within an acceptable time period.[15] This will not be an easy task. New studies are already casting doubt on the feasibility of this goal, warning that continuing problems including deforestation[16], and the existing energy infrastructure of the world[17], will see us exceed this target.
- Climate change poses very real threats to humans and to civilization that are not just in the future, but are happening right now. The impact on the military is described in the US Department of Defense (DOD) Climate-Related Risk to DOD Infrastructure Initial Vulnerability Assessment Survey, is sobering.[18]
- Climate change is already having an impact on human health – and it's not limited to just weather.
  - A 2011 study found that estimated health costs of six climate-change related events exceeded $14 billion (2008 dollars)[19]

---

[15] Intergovernmental Panel on Climate Change, "Summary for Policymakers of IPCC Special Report On Global Warming of 1.5C approved by governments"
[16]Calum Brown et al, *Nature*, "Achievement of Paris climate goals unlikely due to time lags in the land system"
[17]Dan Tong et al, *Nature*, "Committed emissions from existing energy infrastructure jeopardize 1.5C climate target"
[18] Homeland Security Digital Library, "Climate-Related Risk to DoD Infrastructure Initial Vulnerability Assessment Survey Report"

⍰ Climate change impacts sea levels and can flood coastal areas. States which have seen the greatest loss due to coastal flooding, and are poised to see even more include Florida, New York, New Jersey and the Carolinas.[20] Some of the cities most threatened with flooding by climate change will include: Galveston, Miami Beach, Miramar, Ocean City, Hilton Head Island, and Charleston.[21]

Third Force Ideas

Here's the first Third Force idea of about climate change and the debate over whether or not we are causing it.

Ready?

IT DOESN'T MATTER!

The fact is, climate change is happening. No matter what is causing it, we have to deal with it.

The Third Force Ideas:

Third Force Idea #1: Come together and adopt a plan and invest in our planet for ourselves and the future by stopping the human activity that may contribute to

---

[19] Knowlton K et al, *PubMed*, "Six climate change-related events in the United States accounted for about $14 billion in lost lives and health costs"

[20] First Street Foundation, "Rising Seas Erode $15.8 Billion in Home Value from Maine to Mississippi"

[21] Zillow & Climate Central, "More Than 386,000 Homes at Risk of Coastal Flooding by 2050"

climate change, planning for these changes that we cannot control, and setting up programs that bring solutions to this new reality.

<u>Third Force Idea #2:</u> Figure out how many trees need to be planted in the world over the next 10 years and allot the trees by the size of each country in the world. Mobilize globally to plant these trees. To avoid losses to the food supply, plant fruit and nut trees. Encourage people to grow some of their own food.

For example, a new study by Swiss economists says that planting 1.2 trillion new trees could negate 10 years of CO_2 emissions[22]....

There are a myriad of other options that will help our planet and the survival of the human species. This course of action assures our future as human beings, and it creates huge economic opportunities for our country.

The Obligations:

<u>Obligation #1:</u> Recognize that one person's right to use natural resources for financial gain is superseded by the harm that might be done to people today and for generations to come.

---

[22] YaleEnvironment360, "Planting 1.2 Trillion Trees Could Cancel Out a Decade of CO2 Emissions, Scientists Find"

<u>Obligation #2:</u> Recognize that regardless of the reason for it, climate change is threatening our way of life and we need a solution.

The Roadmap:

- Set the intention – What do we want the climate and planet Earth to be like?
- Find the commonly accepted terminology that will be mutually accepted in discussion. For example, "securing our future". Our goal is to protect our future by being responsible stewards of our world. We need to turn crises – climate change – into opportunities for new energy sources, healthier food, better water purification systems.
- Find and support leaders who understand the problem and have practical solutions.
- Change our lives, our patterns of consumption, our thinking to lessen the impact of our existence on earth and in our neighborhoods.
- Join with others to make positive environmental and climate change.

Exercise for Chapter 8

1. List your ideas for ways to combat the dangerous effects of climate change.

_____

_____

_____

_____

_____

_____

_____

_____

2. How could we better explain the dangers of climate change to those who don't see it as a threat?

_____

_____

_____

_____

_____

_____

_____

"Will it be possible to maintain a fair standard of living for our own people while helping to raise economic standards in other parts of the world? Not only must it be possible, it must be done! If there will be any lasting peace! But it must begin in the hearts and minds of individuals."

– Edgar Cayce (3976-28)

Chapter 9

Rich One, Poor One Part I: Re-evaluating Free Enterprise

Yes, we said at the beginning that "Magenta Nation" wasn't about academics, charts and graphs. For this one chapter, we're breaking that rule and sharing some graphs with you – because pictures tell stories and what these pictures tell is just downright amazing.

So, what did you buy with the big tax refund you got after the 2017 tax cuts? Well, if you're at the bottom of the economic ladder, you might have purchased a designer coffee. If you're at the top, you might have bought a fully equipped luxury car.

That's right – high income Americans received a tax cut that, percentage-wise, was 10 TIMES that of poorer Americans. Considering that their incomes are so much higher in the first place, that translates into tens of thousands of dollars in refunds – as opposed to the price of a mocha latte for the working-class poor.

The GOP Tax Bill's Estimated Effects In 2018

In 2018, the Republican tax overhaul would give all of these income groups a tax cut, on average. But both by percentages and total dollars, the benefits would be far greater for higher-income households. Households making $1 million or more per year would get an average tax cut of $69,660, a 3.3 percent boost in after-tax income.

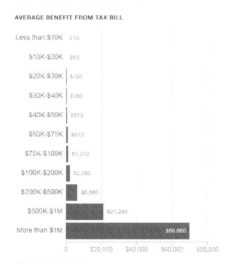

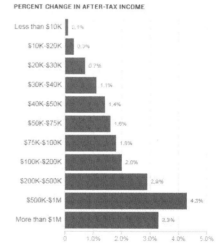

Source: Tax Policy Center

Credit: Danielle Kurtzleben & Katie Park/NPR

23

---

23 Tax Policy Center, "Distributional Analysis of the Conference Agreement for the Tax Cuts and Jobs Act"

Hmm, looks like this great financial boon was smoke and mirrors for us, the average Americans.

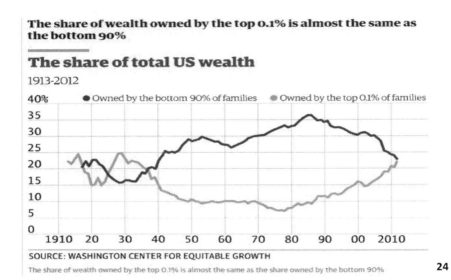

The share of wealth owned by the top 0.1% is almost the same as the bottom 90%

The share of total US wealth

1913-2012

40% ● Owned by the bottom 90% of families   ◉ Owned by the top 0.1% of families

SOURCE: WASHINGTON CENTER FOR EQUITABLE GROWTH

The share of wealth owned by the top 0.1% is almost the same as the share owned by the bottom 90%   **24**

Seeing the reality of America's wealth distribution today is important to understand why we are struggling so much to achieve a standard of living that seemed so easy for our grandparents.

Starting about the time of the trickle-down economics theory a generation ago, more and more of America's wealth has been concentrated in fewer and fewer people. Today, it is concentrated in fewer people than at any time since – you guessed it – just prior to the stock market crash in 1929. In 1929, the wealthiest Americans received 23.9% of U.S. income. In 1975, it was 8.9%. In 2013, it was back to 22%.

---

[24] Angela Monaghan, *The Guardian*, "US wealth inequality—top 0.1% worth as much as the bottom 90%"

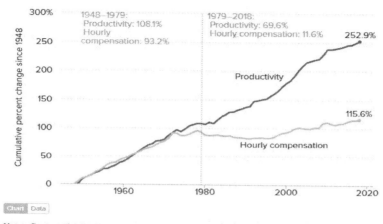

The gap between productivity and a typical worker's compensation has increased dramatically since 1979

Productivity growth and hourly compensation growth, 1948–2018

Chart axis: Cumulative percent change since 1948

1948–1979:
Productivity: 108.1%
Hourly compensation: 93.2%

1979–2018:
Productivity: 69.6%
Hourly compensation: 11.6%

252.9%

Productivity

115.6%

Hourly compensation

Chart | Data

Notes: Data are for compensation (wages and benefits) of production/nonsupervisory workers in the private sector and net productivity of the total economy. "Net productivity" is the growth of output of goods and services less depreciation per hour worked.

Source: EPI analysis of unpublished Total Economy Productivity data from Bureau of Labor Statistics (BLS) Labor Productivity and Costs program, wage data from the BLS Current Employment Statistics, BLS Employment Cost Trends, BLS Consumer Price Index, and Bureau of Economic Analysis National Income and Product Accounts

25

It's not just in taxes that the average American is getting the short end of the stick. The productivity of our workforce has gone up and up, but wages have not. As a reward for our industriousness, the purchasing power of wages has actually gone down. Since 1973, while productivity has tripled, wages have dropped.

Since President Eisenhower's time as president in the 1950's, the tax rate for the wealthy has dropped from 91% to 39.6%.[26] Rich people are getting more money and

---

[25] Economic Policy Institute: "The Productivity—Pay Gap"

[26] *PolitiFact*, "Income tax rates were 90 percent under Eisenhower, Sanders says"

paying less taxes, while the average American is working harder for less.

The myth of trickle-down economics, which took hold during the Reagan era, is in part responsible for this Grand Canyon-like chasm between the rich and the rest of us. "Trickle-down economics" refers to targeted tax cuts to wealthier individuals/entities over more across-the-board tax cuts in supply-side economics. The idea is that reduced taxes for rich people and corporations will turn into increased economic growth as the money is reinvested in the economy.

After 35 years, the results are in on the effectiveness of this theory. Instead of helping everyone, these policies disproportionately benefited the wealthy. From 1979-2005, after-tax household income rose by 6% for the bottom fifth of Americans. The top fifth saw an 80% increase – more than 11 times the increase than that experienced by the working poor. The top 1% had their income tripled.[27]

In 1965, CEO pay was 20 times that of a typical American worker. In 2016, CEO pay was 271 times[28] that of the average employed American. In 50 years, the gap between the pay for average Americans and CEOs increased by 1,250 %.

[27] Kimberly Amadeo, *The Balance*, "Why Trickle-Down Economics Works in Theory But Not in Fact"

[28] Carmen Reinicke, *CNBC*, "US income inequality continues to grow"

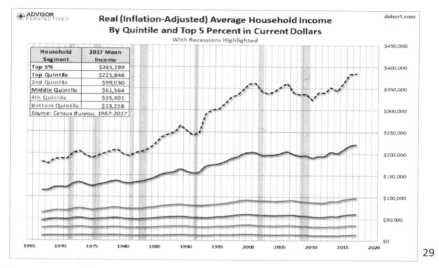

Real (Inflation-Adjusted) Average Household Income
By Quintile and Top 5 Percent in Current Dollars
With Recessions Highlighted

Household Segment	2017 Mean Income
Top 5%	$385,289
Top Quintile	$221,846
2nd Quintile	$99,030
Middle Quintile	$61,564
4th Quintile	$35,401
Bottom Quintile	$13,258
Source: Census Bureau, 1967-2017	

In terms of economic well-being, the average American flat-lined. In contrast, people who were wealthy are now mega wealthy.

It's a clear, obvious answer to the average American and the working poor who wonder, "Why am I working so hard and have so much less?"

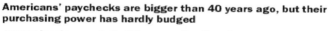

Americans' paychecks are bigger than 40 years ago, but their purchasing power has hardly budged

Average hourly wages in the U.S., seasonally adjusted

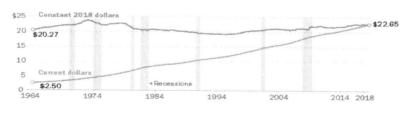

Source: U.S. Bureau of Labor Statistics.

Pew Research Center

[29] Jill Mislinski, Advisor Perspectives, "U.S. Household Incomes: A 50+ Year Perspective"

[30] Drew Desilver, *Pew Research Center*, "For most U.S. workers, real wages have barely budged in decades"

After considering these economic facts about where America's wealth goes, think about the costs that the average American must earn and pay for: health care, a college education, retirement. Then ask yourself how anyone can say "we can't afford health care for everybody," "we can't afford to make college costs within reach of everyone," "we can't afford to keep our promise to older Americans to provide health care and a living stipend in their retirement" when our nation's wealth is hoarded by a few elite individuals and the rest of us are sliding down the economic slope, continually working harder for less.

The truth is we CAN afford those things, IF the majority of Americans decide these needs are more important than helping megajillionnaires acquire more millions.

The Third Force Ideas

Third Force Idea #1: Face up to the truth that for forty years, economic and government policy has been misused to benefit the wealthy at the expense of everyone else. Over and over again, the promises that "tax cuts" and "reduced government regulation of business" would make everyone rich, is a lie. Stop believing the lie. Believe the facts and the reality that everyday Americans are facing. Suck it up and be prepared to make some serious re-adjustments.

Third Force Idea # 2: Recognize that unfettered capitalism does not work in the modern age. Good-hearted billionaires cannot be relied on to take care of us. For the most part, they will only take care of themselves. Yes, there are wealthy people with consciences who donate huge amounts to charity and to address the world's inequities. But rather than one-off solutions, we need systems and solutions coming together to address the root causes of inequity and to fix them.

Third Force Idea #3: Develop a plan for redistribution of wealth so that the average American is not short-changed in terms of financial well-being. Free up funds so that those items that are so expensive to the average American can be affordable. Stop being frightened by the boogieman of "higher taxes" or "socialism". Since when is financial security a bad thing?

The Obligation: To those whom much is given, much is expected. Americans should give back to society at the level they are receiving from it. If someone has become wealthy in America, they have a HUGE obligation to give back to America for the privilege of living in the free enterprise economy that made their success possible. Taxes are viewed as evil by many who must pay them, but they are actually an investment into the society that made it possible for people to become better off financially.

The Roadmap

- Set the intention – What is our ideal for the financial future of America and Americans?

- Determine the terminology that will bring us together, such as a level economic playing field for all to achieve sustainable prosperity and financial security.
- Educate Americans in the truth of economics today, and separate "making rich people richer" from "the right of every person to pursue economic success."
- Establish equity in taxation for wealthy individuals and corporations and the rest of America.
- Establish a plan for this revenue to be channeled into programs that benefit all Americans.

Exercise for Chapter 9

If America had a more equitable distribution of wealth, how would it change our country?

_____

_____

_____

_____

_____

_____

_____

Chapter 10

Rich One, Poor One Part II: Should Americans Ever Be Poor?

Screaming fights. Crying children. Slamming doors.

The changing dynamics at the apartment building next to my newly-acquired townhouse made me nervous. What was up? Well, unbeknownst to me, the building had been transformed into subsidized housing.

Unfortunately, the apartment complex was directly beyond the window of my parents' "room" where they stayed when they came on frequent visits. Now firmly in the senior citizen category, they made no secret of how important sleep was to their well-being.

So, Mom and Dad arrived, and I decided not to say anything, hoping for the best. But sure enough, the second day of their visit, my father asked me, "What's up with the building next door?"

Uh oh. I waited for the complaints – noisy, can't sleep, unexpected outbursts in the night. But Dad just looked at me and said, "Those children have no place to play."

So that was his concern – the children who had no yard, only a 4x4 foot concrete slab in front of their unit. Another lesson that Dad opened my eyes to was what was really important – not the inconvenience of some noise, but children who sat on the stoop waiting for their parents to return from work with nothing to do but argue, get into mischief and waste their time.

As I've said before in this book, Dad was a successful businessman. He was also a standout member of the Silent Generation. Hard work mattered – but so did compassion. He saw the human side of the situation, not just the inconvenience to him. His attitude changed my view as well.

The Positions: While patriarchs do not hate poor people, they are more likely to view poverty as an ultimately self-inflicted status. If someone is poor, they may see it as a result of a character deficit or a lack of initiative. Poor people may be seen as "takers" who limit others by soaking up resources through social safety net programs. Patriarchs may support limited social safety programs that give temporary help but are distrusting of too many programs that create a cycle of dependence on the government.

Communitarians are more likely to view poverty as a situation of circumstances, and less like a representation of character (or lack of). They acknowledge that poverty often happens in temporary cycles – many people are not perpetually impoverished – and is emblematic of a need for a quick helping hand. At the same time, there are systemic forces that tend to perpetuate a multi-generational quagmire of impoverished circumstances, fueled by racism, ill health and lack of education.

Relevant Facts

- ☐ An estimated 12.3% of Americans lived in poverty in 2017 - 39.7 million people[31]
    - More than 15 million of these people are children (21% of American children, or one out of every five children) living in households earning incomes below the federal poverty threshold[32]
    - 31% of those in poverty are adults not working
    - 26% are single moms
    - 25% are adults with disabilities
    - 25% are adults without high school diplomas
    - 21% are African Americans
    - 18% are Latinos
    - 12% are single dads[33]
- ☐ In 2015, an estimated 21.3% of Americans – 52.2 million people – were participating in government assistance programs every month[34]

The "wealth gap" not only economically challenges the middle class, but helps keep a steadily increasing percentage of Americans in poverty.

---

[31] J. Semega et al, UC Davis Center for Poverty Research, "What is the current poverty rate in the United States?"

[32] National Center For Children in Poverty, "Child Poverty"

[33] Federal Safety Net, "U.S. Poverty Statistics"

[34] US Census Bureau, "21.3 Percent of U.S. Population Participates in Government Assistance Programs Each Month"

Let's look for a moment at the impact of these economic realities on the American family and on the children, who are our future.

Except for the affluent, it is almost impossible today for an American family to survive unless both parents work. Two working parents means significant stress on time with the family. While many parents make extraordinary sacrifices to achieve this quality time, it's hard and very stressful – hard on both mental and physical health to live with these conflicting agendas and inadequate sleep.

For the family in poverty, adults may be working two or more jobs. How can they devote the time necessary to properly parent, however much they try?

Their children are therefore more susceptible to the temptations of finding a community elsewhere. Sometimes they are fortunate and find it in a church, school, or other nurturing environments. Sometimes it is found in gangs, drugs, sexual promiscuity, alcohol, or crime.

The Truth About Children Raised in Poverty

These family issues fueled by economics are why doctors and therapists may stop asking *"What's wrong with you,"* and instead will inquire *"What happened to you?"*. A report from the American Academy of Pediatrics, the Center for Disease Control and Prevention, and Kaiser Permanente shows adverse childhood events could bring significant and negative adult physical and mental health outcomes affecting more than 60% of adults.[35] What children experience shapes their ability to be economically stable, employed, healthy, and to be good parents to their own children.

What are adverse childhood experiences? They include:
- Emotional abuse
- Physical abuse
- Sexual abuse
- Emotional neglect
- Physical neglect
- Mother treated violently
- Household substance abuse
- Household mental illness
- Parental separation or divorce
- Incarcerated household member

Adverse childhood experiences (ACEs) occur regularly with children aged 0 to 18 years across all races, economic classes, and geographic regions; however, there is a much higher prevalence of ACEs for those living in poverty.

While some stress in life is normal – and even necessary for development – the type of stress that results when a child experiences ACEs may become toxic when there is "strong, frequent, or prolonged activation of the body's stress response systems in the absence of the buffering

---

[35] Vincent J. Felitti et al, *American Journal of Preventive Medicine*, "Relationship of Childhood Abuse and Household Dysfunction to Many of the Leading Causes of Death in Adults"

protection of a supportive, adult relationship."[36] The biological response to this toxic stress can be incredibly destructive and last a lifetime. It is as if the person has a permanent case of Post-traumatic Stress Disorder (PTSD).

The Input of ACE's and Poverty

Researchers have found many of the most common adult life-threatening health conditions, including obesity, heart disease, alcoholism, and drug use are directly related to childhood adversity. A child who has experienced ACEs is more likely to have learning and behavioral issues and is at higher risk for early initiation of sexual activity and adolescent pregnancy. These effects can be magnified through generations if the traumatic experiences are not addressed. The financial cost to individuals and society is enormous.

But the impact of poverty extends far beyond money. It is behind many of the systemic ills that plague our society – drugs, crime, incarceration, unemployment, mental and physical illness. And these crises are not attributed to character flaws. They have a basis in biology, and are related to the chronic stress of poverty, racism, and abuse. Poverty is a social problem that wastes huge economic resources and costs us far more than would curing it.

---

[36] Jessica Barreca, American Physical Therapy Association: "Understanding Trauma and Chronic Toxic Stress in Your Pediatric Patients"

Eliminating poverty will help curtail many negative childhood experiences that handicap children for life. When a person grows up in a household where anger is expressed with violence, this is what they carry into adulthood.

When parents must work three jobs to survive and cannot consistently supervise their children, those children are more likely to get into trouble. If the pain of life is so great that drugs or alcohol is the only option to numb it, children learn these behaviors as a coping mechanism.

ACE's are hardly confined to families living in poverty, yet they are more likely to occur there. Protecting and nurturing children so they grow up to become healthy adults isn't just about having money. It is about growing up with loving adults who are good role models. It is about learning the skills that are labeled as "emotional intelligence" to rise out of poverty in other ways.

If every child had this kind of upbringing, think about the results: In one generation, we could eliminate so much pain and suffering, stop the waste of resources and human lives, and create a much safer world for everyone.

The Third Force Ideas

Third Force Idea #1: Eliminate poverty by investing in our work force and our future; we don't need a "safety net" but an "enablement ladder" to bring people out of poverty. Over time, this investment will eliminate the need for much of the traditional safety net.

Third Force Idea #2: Protect all of us from the ills of poverty and deprivation by eliminating the ways Americans can fall into poverty – through illness, old age, and family obligations that exceed income. For example, the majority of bankruptcies filed in the U.S. cite an instance of severe illness that precipitated it.[37]

If part of our wealth provided health care, education through college that prepared students for employment, basic housing when needed, and more livable retirement, we could all enjoy freedom from worry about earning these items ourselves. American businesses and companies would get an incredible competitive boost if they no longer had to provide employee health care.

Third Force Idea #3: Require mandatory employment for those who can work. No one needs to be unemployed in America. Our needs are so great – in maintaining our infrastructure, our schools, our health care systems, taking care of the elderly and disabled, fighting environmental dangers – that there is a place for every adult capable of working. And as we work together, we build relationships, understanding that people who may seem "different" are really like us.

---

[37] Lorie Konish, *CNBC*, "This is the real reason most Americans file for bankruptcy"

When talking about mandating work, keep in mind that the majority of people receiving public assistance are children, or they are disabled. These people can't work. Caretaking and supporting them are humanitarian efforts, and are investments in the future.

Third Force Idea #4: Have zero tolerance for adult behavior that causes adverse childhood events, which are shown to be contributing factors for illness, poverty, and crime. These situations are not limited to households in poverty, and this solution must extend throughout our nation. If families are not able to provide the nurturing and guidance children need, it must be found elsewhere.

The Obligations

Obligation #1: Those who are helped owe America for their privilege. If they are not paying taxes, they should contribute by being part of work programs, community service, or even mandatory service as young adults.

Obligation #2: No adult has the right to act in such a way as to create adverse childhood events for children. We ALL pay for the consequences as these children grow up.

Does Money Make Us Happy?

Before we leave this topic, let's look at what truly makes people happy and the relationship of happiness to security.

Unfortunately, America does not rank high on the happiness scale. This is contrary to the attitudes that most Americans have that this is the greatest country on earth, and we have more benefits than any other nation.

The ten happiest nations in the world include Finland, Norway, Denmark, Iceland, Switzerland and the Netherlands.[38]

The countries were also ranked among the ten most productive countries in the world in 2018:[39]

So, these countries are doing very well financially, and have citizens who are happy. What's that about? And these happy countries have ice, snow, and freezing temperatures most of the year! What is with these people?

Does that mean economic wealth equates to happiness? If that were true, the U.S. should top the list. Instead, these results infer that economic security equates to happiness. It also shows that countries that provide their citizens with economic security can also be top economic performers.

The one thing the citizens of these nations all have in common is this: they are free from the fear of falling into poverty while trying to provide for their basic needs.

---

[38] World Happiness Report, "World Happiness Report 2018"

[39] Melanie Dimmitt, Expert Market, "15 of the World's Most Productive Countries"

- They will not go bankrupt if they get sick.
- They will not eat cat food when they are old.
- They will not be chained to six figure debts for having the audacity to want a college education.
- They have paid parental leave and help when children are young so that families are not penalized for reproducing. And those children are secure and looked after, setting them on the road to success.

Do these citizens miss their "freedom" to make their way in the world solely from their own resources?

Apparently not.

Are their economies suffering from high taxes? Are their entrepreneurs stifled? Apparently not.

Yes, it is possible to have creativity, a robust economy, and the safety of having one's basic needs met.

Back to Rich Man, Poor Man. So, the road to economic security for all Americans can support economic success for everyone.

The Roadmap

- Set the intention – What is our intention for economic health for all Americans?
- Determine the terminology that will bring us together. "Enable everyone to contribute to

America's economy. Require those who benefit
from America to contribute to America".
- Build the "enablement ladder", community by
community.
- Surround children with a community structure to
ensure they become healthy, functioning adults.

Exercise for Chapter 10

1. If we did have an enablement ladder to lift people out
of poverty, what would it look like?

_____

_____

_____

_____

_____

_____

_____

_____

Chapter 11

Health Care: Right or Privilege?

Is it medically possible to slip an egg under your skin? Well, that's what it looked like had happened to me.

The hard, immovable lump on my calf was the size of an egg. Not a pigeon egg, or a quail egg, but an egg from a good-sized hen or even a turkey. The sheer size of it stretched the skin, and looked like it might burst at any moment. Can anyone say "Alien?"

At the time, I was in Scotland attending a program. I showed this phenomenon around to the facilitators, and after they, too, gasped in horror, there was mutual agreement that this aberration needed medical attention. So, I traveled with one of the coordinators to a clinic in the tiny village of Forres, Scotland.

From the outside, it looked like any medical group office. We approached the desk that was "manned" by three people and explained the situation. I knew health care, I understood about the National Health Service that provided free health care for all residents of the UK. As an American, I did not qualify. So, I offered my insurance card. They examine it, completely mystified.

"Will my insurance cover this visit?" I asked. "Or, if not, how much should I pay you?"

I might as well have been speaking Swahili. They exchanged glances, then said, "Let's get you seen and then we can talk about it."

We sat down in a cheery waiting room where the names of patients and the room they were assigned flashed across an electronic message board. I barely had time to ask my companion about health care in his native country, the Netherlands, when I was called to Room 6.

Behind a privacy curtain, a lady who identified herself as a nurse practitioner examined my leg, asked me questions, cleaned it, and provided medication. "Extreme reaction to an insect bite," was the diagnosis.

In 30 minutes, I was treated and released. Stopping back at the desk, I again asked about payment. They just smiled as if to say "Crazy American," and said there was no charge.

A minor incident, you say? Not enough upon which to base an opinion? Here's another situation, much more serious.

An American lady had a heart attack on a remote Scottish island. The paramedics were there in minutes. Treated first at the local hospital, she was air evacuated to Glasgow, where a nurse was assigned to her and actually flew back with her to the United States. The cost? Nothing.

I work in health care, and I well understand that the situation in the U.S. would have been very different. Yes, both patients would have gotten care. There would have been costs associated with that care, and probably the response would not have been as prompt. I might have had to wait to see my doctor. Seeking care in the ER is expensive. And I don't even know the urgent care center closest to me.

The lady with the heart attack would probably have had to wait longer in a rural area of America for those paramedics. There would be a gaggle of specialists around her bed, ordering lots of tests and running up lots of bills. She would definitely have a hefty price to pay for the inconvenience of having a medical emergency on holiday, in a remote area away from home.

Finally, consider the story of the American student in Taiwan that was shared virally 200,000 times and reported in the *Washington Post*[40]. Suffering from stomach pains, he went to the ER where he was treated promptly and billed $80. Had he had Taiwanese health insurance, the cost would have been less. Ironically, since he had no insurance in the U.S., had he gone to an American ER the cost probably would have been in the thousands of dollars.

The Positions

---

[40] Eli Rosenberg, *The Washington Post*, "An American got sick in Taiwan. He came back with a tale of the 'horrors of socialized medicine'"

The opposing views about health care in this country can be boiled down into two conflicting beliefs:

- ☐ Health care is a commodity, subject to marketplace forces.
- ☐ Health care is a right, necessary for the pursuit of liberty and happiness.

The History of Health: Two Paths Diverge

After World War II, when Europe was in ruins, millions of people were displaced, and millions more had been murdered or killed in combat, the countries there did a very strange thing.

They decided to provide free health care to everyone.

Why, with no money or resources, did they decide to do this?

It was because they believe that the health of their citizens was essential to rebuilding their nations, and to their future.

The U.S. had not suffered such deprivation during the war. It did not make this decision about health care.

At various times, the prospect of a national health care system in the U.S. has been considered. But Americans' distaste for government involvement in their lives – and the opposition of the medical establishment – stymied any progress in that direction.

Instead, the provision of health care in America became the responsibility of employers. Starting with labor unions who wanted health care coverage for their members, and spreading throughout America, employers today provide the majority of health care coverage for working-age Americans and their dependents. A patchwork quilt of insurers, medical providers and administrators provide care in what is considered a "healthcare marketplace."

Another version of that health care marketplace provides coverage and care for seniors, and those in need, through Medicare and Medicaid.

The Results – Not Good Enough

Many Americans believe that our system of health care is the best in the world.

Well, not so fast.

The Commonwealth Fund study, "Mirror, Mirror 2017: International Comparison Reflects Flaws and Opportunities for Better U.S. Health Care", looked at health care metrics for 11 Western nations: Australia, Canada, France, Germany, the Netherlands, New Zealand, Norway, Sweden, Switzerland, the United Kingdom, and the United States. It reports:

"The U.S. ranked last on (health care) performance overall, and ranked last or near last on the Access,

Administrative Efficiency, Equity, and Health Care Outcomes domains. The top ranked countries overall were the U.K., Australia, and the Netherlands. Based on a broad range of indicators, the U.S. health system is an outlier, spending far more but falling short of the performance achieved by other high-income countries. The results suggest the U.S. health care system should look at other countries' approaches if it wants to achieve an affordable high-performing health care system that serves all Americans."

For all the money we spend on health care, we are not getting the value we should. The U.S. has the worst child mortality rate out of twenty countries as reported in the Organisation for Economic Co-operation and Development[41]. Our average life expectancy is dropping[42]. American women are more likely to perish from pregnancy complications than women in any other developed nation[43]. We have a highly sophisticated system of medical technology, but a high rate of medical errors and infection. Our system is fragmented. Providers are paid by services, not outcomes. And the cost is one of the highest in the world.[44]

---

[41] David Johnson, *Time*, "American Babies Are Less Likely to Survive Their First Year Than Babies In Other Rich Countries"

[42] Olga Khazan, *The Atlantic*, "Americans Are Dying Even Younger: Drug overdoses and suicides are causing American life expectancy to drop"

[43] Nina Martin, *NPR*, "U.S. Has the Worst Rate of Maternal Deaths in the Developed World"

[44] Ray Sipherd, *CNBC*, "The third-leading cause of death in US most doctors don't want you to know about"

Here's an example. In my business I paid the full cost of health care for my employees long after other companies had resorted to "cost sharing" to save money. For myself, my husband, and my two children, the cost per year for insurance was $40,000. That's right – no misplaced zeroes here. And we were all perfectly healthy.

When compared to other similar countries, America pays more, yet has worse health results than most other Westernized nations. Why is this?[45]

You may wonder, how can we spend so much of our GDP on health care, and not get our money's worth?

The fact is, you can't win the Indianapolis 500 driving a Model T.

Our system needs to be re-designed and how health care is paid for needs to change. The marketplace of health care is a fallacy. Who can live without health? Who can pursue happiness without health?

Succinctly put, the reason why other countries pay less for health care and get more is that their systems are coordinated – providers are incentivized to work together, not compete for payment.

And in other countries, health care is more broadly available, whereas in the U.S., many people who are poor

---

[45] Karen Feldscher, *The Harvard Gazette*, "What's behind high U.S. health care costs"

or unemployed or whose employers don't offer insurance, just don't get health care. When they need services on an emergency basis, it drives up the total cost for everyone. The 2014 "Mirror, Mirror," report says:

"The U.S. stands apart from other industrialized countries because it does not offer universal health insurance, meaning lower income individuals often don't have sufficient access to health care – especially preventive medicine – compared with other countries. . . . The lower the performance score for equity, the lower the performance on other measures. This suggests that, when a country fails to meet the needs of the most vulnerable, it also fails to meet needs for the average citizen."

Can Americans ingenuity construct a similar, coordinated system? Of course we can. We just need to want to do it.

Relevant Facts:

- America spends almost 18% of its gross national product on health care.[46]
- American households paid $365.5 billion out of their pockets for health services in 2017, ten percent of national expenditures on healthcare.[47] That's more than $1,000 for every man, woman and child. And this does NOT include insurance premiums.

---

[46] Centers for Medicare & Medicaid Services, "National Health Expenditure Data: Historical"
[47] Centers for Medicare and Medicaid Services, "National Health Expenditure Data: NHE Fact Sheet"

- The average cost of an insurance premium for an American worker is $6,896. Employers pay approximately 82% of that cost, with the employees themselves shouldering the remaining 18%.[48]

Polls show that most Americans today favor health coverage for all[49]. Some say the cost is too high. <u>But in reality, we are already paying that high cost.</u>

How We Pay Now

Today, 74 million people are on Medicaid, the program provided by states for low-income Americans. We as taxpayers pay for it. Of Medicaid enrollees, 15% are seniors. And 36 million children are covered by Medicaid and the Children's Health program.

Do we want children and seniors to get health care? Do we want healthy Americans, even if they are poor? Yes, of course. The fact is we're already paying MORE than if this care was provided without the piecemeal system of health care today. Make it available to all, and that care can be managed. Costs for administering the financial part of the system will go down. Quality will go up.

Employers also hire companies to help them manage benefits, keep employees healthy and productive and lower the cost of the program. What if all this

---

[48] John Tozzi, *Insurance Journal*, "Employees' Share of Health Costs Continues Rising Faster Than Wages"
[49] Yoni Blumberg, *CNBC*, "70% of Americans now support Medicare-for-All—here's how single payer could affect you"

administration went off the balance sheet for American companies? What a relief! What a global competitive advantage! And what a cost savings if health care could be provided without the cumbersome apparatus that currently exists to help employers manage care.

OK, I can hear the objections. What about the stories of waits for procedures in other countries? What about waits in the U.S.? According to the Health System Tracker question, "How does the quality of the U.S. healthcare system compare to other countries?" reports that adults in other Western countries have quicker access to a doctor or nurse when they need care than do people in the U.S. In 2017, it took an average of 24 days to schedule a new patient-physician appointment in 15 of America's largest cities.[50]

Some argue that there is a tax burden on the citizens of other countries that must be raised to pay for health care services. Well, don't we as Americans pay that now? $40,000 a year for insurance for a healthy family of four is outrageous. That's more than many families make in a year.

And what about the burden on employers? What if that cost were paid by a tax, and they were free of the burden of trying to manage the health of their employees?

There's a strong dollars and cents argument for a more coordinated, centralized system for American health care

---

[50] Merritt Hawkins, "2017 Survey of Physician Appointment Wait Times"

delivery, as well as the improvements in quality that would results if care was delivered by coordinated, connected systems.

Are Other Countries Just "Different"?

There's a school of thought that other nations have universal health care coverage because they are just raised to be altruistic, while Americans are individualists who want to do things for themselves. The idea of health care for all just doesn't fit with our values.

Europeans don't see this decision as altruistic. They see it as practical. They even see it as selfish. It's clear to them that the benefits for having health care for everyone accrue to everyone. It's the only sensible choice.

Many Americans have an innate distrust of government to run any large enterprise. They don't want to trust health care to a central authority. However, undeniably, it is working for most of the rest of the industrialized world to provide better health care at a lower cost and a higher level of quality and efficiency.

In the U.S., the Americans most satisfied with their health care receive Medicare, which is run by the government[51]. The Post Office, the military, and the treasury are among the many functions we rely on government to manage – and their operation is not questioned.

---

[51] Justin McCarthy, *Gallup News*, "Most Americans Still Rate Their Healthcare Quite Positively"

Many stakeholders in health care have strong economic reasons to fight for the status quo. However, when the choice is whether or not Americans have good health care, these interests will have to compromise. It will be a serious dislocation, but there are models in existence that are succeeding to provide health care with a collaborative, not competitive, system in place. It can be done.

The Third Force Ideas

<u>Third Force Idea #1:</u> Health care is a right. We really cannot pursue liberty and happiness without it. And if it is available to everyone, we will actually save money by keeping people healthy versus performing expensive crisis interventions or having individuals require extensive treatments for conditions that could be prevented.

<u>Third Force Idea #2:</u> The needs of the American people for healthcare must come before those of special interest economic groups.

The Obligation: People are responsible to behave in such a way that they do not invite sickness or injury. If they do, there may be penalties.

The Roadmap

- Set the intention – What is our vision for the health of Americans?

- Determine the terminology that will bring us together: "Americans need to be healthy to pursue liberty and happiness. A healthy workforce is a competitive advantage for American businesses, while illness resulting from lack of access to health care costs everybody."
- Educate Americas on the truth about the quality of health care in other countries that consider health care a right, and the high level of satisfaction in those countries.
- Develop a plan to transfer monies paid by employers for health care into a centralized program where health care can be coordinated and costs better managed.
- Recognize that there should be limits on the ability of Americans to abuse themselves or destroy their health through their own actions. Here's where accountability comes in. People who engage in behaviors that damage their health, or the health of others, are not free to do so and have the rest of us foot the bill.

Exercise for Chapter 11

What do you think about the idea of "healthcare for all"?

_____

_____

_____

Chapter 12

Education: Sesame Street or Mister Rogers?

In recent years, an unsung but beloved hero in America is getting his well-deserved recognition as a strong – if understated – force for good. Fred Rogers dedicated his life to helping children feel loved, worthy, and safe, in his nationally televised TV show that ran for more than a generation.

Alongside his show, which focused on emotional health and healing, another hugely popular show called Sesame Street taught basic educational skills to these same children.

Which approach is more important in American education today? Should young people learn their ABC's and a traditional curriculum, or are schools responsible for teaching self-esteem and values for living? In a Magenta Nation, which is more important?

The Positions: In the area of education, there is – unlike in health care – the belief that everyone should have access to a certain standard of education. However, there are questions about the efficacy of education as it is provided today to American youth.

There is skepticism in some quarters about the government's ability to manage education. Also, some believe that vouchers should be allowed for families who want to send their children to private schools, religious schools, or to home school them. Others think that this practice would weaken the public school system and subsidize religious beliefs in education.

There are also different perspectives on the purpose of education. Is it to prepare students to enter the workforce and contribute to the economy? Or should students learn behaviors and values that will make them good citizens?

Relevant Facts

- Failures in education make our country less competitive.
- The Program for Internal Student Assessment ranked the US 38th out of 71 nations in math and 24th in science.[52]
- Among the 35 members states of the Organization for Economic Co-operation and Development (OECD), the U.S. ranked 30th in math and 19th in science.
- In 2015, average math scores for 4 - 8 graders fell for the first time since 1990.[53]
- Seven percent of graduating college students have more than $100,000 in student loans; 25% owe $43,000 or more.[54]

---

[52] Drew Desilver, *Pew Research*, "U.S. students' academic achievement still lags that of their peers in many other countries"
[53] Drew Desilver, *Pew Research*, "U.S. students' academic achievement still lags that of their peers in many other countries"
[54] Anthony Cilluffo, *Pew Research*, "5 facts about student loans"

Besides falling performance, there is a disconnect between education and careers in the U.S. The obligation of every person receiving education in America is to use that education to give back to society. Many go through the educational process and are unable to find meaningful work, leaving school without the skills to earn a living. It makes sense that those who seek education must be able to have an alternative track to be employable.

Young Americans must also learn basic skills of good citizenship, how to cooperate, collaborate, make good choices, to make responsible voting choices, and to be responsible employers, family members, and citizens. Where else are they going to learn these behaviors, except in school?

And what about the environment of the school itself? Schools are microcosms of the types of communities that we want to have throughout our country. Applying the value of respect, consideration, compassion and support in the school setting will teach children to live these values as adults.

The truth is, we need both Sesame Street and Mister Rogers in our educational system, a balance of head and heart to produce graduates who can earn a living and be good citizens.

The Third Force Ideas

<u>Third Force Idea #1</u>: View education like the Soviets did in the 1960's, when they led in science and the space race. Identify abilities and aptitudes early on, consider a multiplicity of career options and training, give promotions and opportunities based on merit. The goal is that students should end their education with practical skills to earn a living.

<u>Third Force Idea #2</u>: Rather than stripping values from education, we need to teach more values. The educational system should teach our children the values that we want Americans to have. Everyone is required to learn emotional intelligence, critical thinking and civics. Everyone should be educated to be an intelligent voter. Everyone should be taught how to be a good citizen, to live in a community and to deal with conflict.

<u>Third Force Idea #3</u>: Reduce the cost of college in dollars and require payment in service, post-graduation. Most other First World countries provide free or near free college education. They also skip the two years of general studies that American students are required to take, and go right into their major field of study.

American students of merit, who have demonstrated the ability to benefit from a college education, should have that education without having to go into debt to do so. In return, they are obligated to provide two – four years of service to their country and society – not in the military per se, but in service where the country needs help.

One not-so-obvious benefit of this system will be involving young people with those who are different from themselves – in culture, race and values. "Us" and "them" viewpoints will be softened. And acts of service will foster compassion for people other than themselves.

The Obligations

Obligation #1: Recognize that education is a privilege to prepare the student not only to support themselves, but to contribute back to society. Those who do not want to complete minimal educational requirements are required to join a workforce program to train them in a career and put them to work while doing so.

Obligation #2: All Americans are obligated to learn how their country works and what the issues of the day are so they can be intelligent voters.

Obligation #3: Students who require financial assistance for college can repay that assistance with community service work.

The Roadmap

- Set the intention – What is our vision for the education of America?
- Determine the terminology that will bring us together: Education to have a prosperous, harmonious America.

- Research and expand the public service option to give students the chance to pay for college with service after graduation.
- Develop a value-based curriculum to give students basic skills in relationships, collaboration, and citizenship as part of their education.
- Re-design the public school curriculum to identify aptitudes early on to help students self-select tracks to vocational and career options.
- Begin these programs in impoverished neighborhoods as part of creating the "enablement ladder."

Exercises for Chapter 12

1. What do you think about the ideas for educating Americans in this chapter?

_____

_____

_____

_____

_____

_____

2. What are your ideas?

Chapter 13

Immigration: Melting Pot or Great White Hope?

The great white hope – that's a good description of how Americans viewed their destiny 100 years ago. The tsunami of immigrants from Europe and other countries created a backlash that morphed into a new iteration of the white supremacist movement. It was so well articulated and widespread that Adolph Hitler credited an American eugenics leader with inspiring his theories of the master Aryan race, and how to create one[55].

However, when Hitler went beyond rhetoric and began to execute his ideas for exterminating "mongrels" and achieving military domination, the U.S. responded with a deadly defense of itself and its core values.

Now 100 years later, history is in a sense repeating itself. A global influx of refugees has inundated Western Europe and the southern part of the U.S. These refugees are viewed by some with suspicion, fear and anger, as a threat to the American Way, to America's prosperity, and sometimes, to American lives.

The Immigration and Nationality Act of 1952 defined how the current system of immigration works:
- Ended the exclusion of Asian peoples from immigration to the U.S.

---

[55] Edwin Black, *The Guardian*, "Hitler's Debt to America"

- Established the core principles of American immigration as: family reunification, bolstering the US economy with skilled individuals, protecting refugees and increasing diversity.

Do these principles work today? That's the debate.

The Position: Today there are two perspectives on immigration. One is that immigrants are dangerous. They might be terrorists or gangsters, and probably are. They want to live off of us and deplete our resources without contributing to our society. Their differences are a threat to the American way of life.

The opposite perspective sees immigrants as necessary to the well-being of this country. We're all immigrants, even Native Americans. We need a pathway for people to enter this country and become citizens. The differences in immigrants' culture make America richer, not poorer. And we need to recognize that many immigrants are refugees – fleeing starvation, persecution and threats to their lives. As the standard-bearer for justice in the world, America must stand up for the oppressed everywhere.

Relevant Facts:

- Currently there are 44.4 million immigrants in the U.S., 13.6% of the American population. More than one in ten Americans is an immigrant.[56]

---

[56] Jynnah Radford, *Pew Research Center*, "Key findings about US immigrants"

- There are an estimated 10.5 million illegal immigrants in the U.S. as of 2017, or about 3% of Americans; 4.9 million from Mexico, and the rest from the "Northern Triangle" countries of Guatemala, El Salvador, Honduras, as well as Asia[57].
- Illegal immigrants are often viewed as a drain on our economy. In fact, illegal immigrants contributed an estimated $13 billion to Social Security in 2010, and pay an estimated $9 billion in payroll taxes annually.[58]
  - Legal immigrants must wait five years before accessing federal public benefits like Medicaid, SNAP, cash assistance and Social Security. Illegal immigrants cannot access these benefits at all.[59]
- Much of the fear about immigrants is driven by concerns that criminals are coming into the country, and that we are in danger. In fact, undocumented immigrants and legal immigrants both have much lower rates of crime than the American citizenry as a whole, with non-immigrants more than four times more likely to be arrested.[60]
- Overall, the American people view immigrants favorably: 74% of Americans favor granting legal status to immigrants brought in illegally as children, and 60% oppose expanding walls along the border.[61]

[57] Jens Manuel Krogstad, Jeffrey Passel, and D'Vera Cohn, *Pew Research Center*, "5 facts about illegal immigration in the US")

[58] Alexia Fernández Campbell, *Vox*, "Trump says undocumented immigrants burden the safety net. He's wrong."

[59] National Immigration Forum, "Fact Sheet: Immigrants and Public Benefits"

[60] The National Academies of Sciences, Engineering, & Medicine, "The Integration of Immigrants into American Society", pg. 7

Third Force Ideas

Third force Idea #1: Acknowledge that immigration is a global issue and look at the causes of why people are fleeing their native lands. There are two main reasons: war and political persecution, and economic disaster sometimes brought on by climate change. These are the real problems that should be addressed.

Third Force Idea #2: Recognize that immigrants have a responsibility to the country that adopts them. There should be work requirements, public service requirements – some type of contribution to their adopted country in return for their right to asylum and citizenship.

Third Force Idea #3: Give illegal immigrants a visa program that would enable them to work, pay taxes, contribute to American society, and be tracked instead of living underground. Again, this program should specify the obligation that these new Americans have to their new country.

The Obligation: Immigrants must give back to the country that adopted them: pay taxes, vote, devote themselves in a formal way to community service. Immigrants seeking asylum should not be treated as criminals.

---

[61] Carroll Doherty, *Pew Research*, "Americans broadly support legal status for immigrants brought to the U.S. illegally as children"

There should be a clearer path for immigrants seeking employment and immigrants seeking asylum to enter the U.S.

The Roadmap

- Set the intention – What is our view of bringing in "new" Americans?
- Determine the terminology that we can all support. A safe immigration policy can impart needed skills to America and provide humanitarian support for refugees, including a requirement to give back to their adopted country.
- Bring together the ideas of America as a haven for immigrants and a place where immigrants have always made significant contributions, with the need for national safety and economic stability.

Exercise for Chapter 13

What are your views on how immigration should be handled?

_____

_____

_____

_____

_____

_____

_____

_____

Chapter 14

Don't Take My Guns Away

"Mommy, I found some toys. Can I play with them?"

My adorable three-year-old looked up at me, his blue eyes beseeching.

Thinking it unlikely that our hosts, my wonderful aunt and uncle who were in their 80's, would have toys, I asked him, "Can you show me?"

He eagerly led me up a winding staircase to the darkened bedroom above. How had he wandered up here and I hadn't even seen him? He got down on his hands and knees, lifted the bedspread, and proudly showed me what he had found.

My breath stopped.

The "toys" were real guns.

"No, Honey, I don't think you can play with those. Come downstairs and I'll play with you. Please don't come up here again. I don't think you should be in this room."

Later, I found a quiet moment to tell my aunt what had happened. Inside, I was still shaking from this near escape. Had my son not been so obedient, he could easily have taken those guns out to inspect, with unspeakably tragic results.

"Yes, I know," she smiled and nodded. Two elderly people, one disabled, miles from the nearest town and law enforcement, living alone. It made sense that they would want something with which to defend themselves, and they would want those weapons close at hand, at night, when the danger was greatest.

But they shouldn't be where my precious child could find them.

The Positions

- ⬚ "Owning guns is a right guaranteed by the Constitution. Taking away guns leaves me defenseless from my enemies, which might just be the government!"
- ⬚ "Gun use in the U.S. is a public health hazard. No other country has the level of gun violence that exists in the U.S. The Constitution is being misread – citizens carrying guns was not the intent of the Founding Fathers."

Gun control is not a black and white issue. For example, Ronald Reagan was one of the first Presidents to defend the perceived Second Amendment rights to gun ownership. In return, the National Rifle Association endorsed him. However, after leaving office, and experiencing being shot himself by a deranged individual, Reagan proposed the Brady Law to establish federal background checks for buyers with criminal records and mental health issues. He also endorsed a ban on assault weapons in 1994.

Relevant Facts

- In the U.S., nearly 13,000 people are murdered by firearms in a year. There are upwards of 370 mass shootings each year in the U.S. and climbing.[62]
- The American gun homicide rate is 25 times higher than other high-income countries.[63]
- When Australia passed gun control, including a buy back of guns, the homicide rate declined by 20% over the following ten years. Between 1989 and 2014, the number of homicide instances involving firearms fell by 57% (Gun control legislation, The National Firearms Agreement, was passed in 1996). There have been no gun massacres since the ban.[64]
- The United Kingdom also saw gun crimes drop sharply after imposing heavy fines or prison terms up to 10 years for possessing illegal firearms.[65]
- Japan has one of the lowest rates of gun ownership globally, reporting six gun deaths in 2014.[66] Since 1958 firearms have been banned except for shotguns; gun owners must attend classes and pass written and practical exams.

---

[62] Dave Mosher & Skye Gould, *Business Insider*, "The odds that a gun will kill the average American may surprise you"

[63] E. Grinshteyn & D. Hemenway, U.S. National Library of Medicine: National Institutes of Health, "Violent Death Rates: The US Compared with Other High-Income OECD Countries, 2010"

[64] Eugene Kiely, *FactCheck.org*, "Gun Control in Australia, updated"

[65] Crown Prosecution Service, "Firearms"

[66] Harry Low, *BBC*, "How Japan has almost eradicated gun crime"

The Third Force Ideas

Third Force Idea #1: One person's perceived rights should never be used as an excuse to harm or endanger others. Accountability for individuals and protecting public safety are the foundation of determining American gun control laws.

Third Force Idea #2: Gun owners are liable for any crimes committed with their guns.

Third Force Idea #3: Words are weapons! Speech that incites or condones violence to others is a weapon and should not be allowed. Those who use such rhetoric are responsible for any harm they may cause. (See Chapter 16)

The Obligations

Obligation #1: People are responsible for damage done with their guns.

Obligation #2: Gun ownership and use by persons who are dangerous and/or with mental health issues should not be allowed.

Obligation #3: Weapons developed for mass killing should never be allowed to be owned by civilians.

The Roadmap

- Set the intention – What is our view of keeping Americans safe from physical and emotional violence? Everyone in America deserves to be safe, especially our young people.
- Determine the terminology that brings us together: Americans deserve a safe environment, especially our young people.
- Prevent dangerous people from owning dangerous guns.
- Establish legal precedent for gun owners to be responsible for damage done to their guns.

Exercises for Chapter 14
1. Why is the debate about gun control so volatile?

_____

_____

_____

_____

_____

_____

_____

2. How could these opposing views come together?

_____

_____

_____

_____

_____

_____

_____

Chapter 15

Finding Our Voice – And Using It

Voting is the most important way to change and renew our country. Why? Well, remember the charts in Chapter 10? At this point in our history, a small group of wealthy individuals and groups have such influence that the deck is stacked against the candidates that people truly want and vote for. Therefore, we need a HUGE majority to make a change.

This goal is a challenge. Americans have a history of not voting at all. Many people don't know the process of registering and voting. Others have transportation barriers, health barriers, and language barriers.

Voter ID laws are confusing. People can be erased from the polling records and find they are not registered after all when they arrive to vote. High rates of incarceration among some races reduce the number of voters from these groups.

But this is a challenge we can win. Instead of feeling daunted, feel empowered. Putting our collective efforts into educating, empowering and motivating voters is the first and most urgent step to revising the American dream.

The Positions: There is unanimity that voting is important. However, there is division on the factors that may keep people from voting. Some don't acknowledge that voter suppression exists. Others are very concerned about it and the misrepresentation it gives to certain groups over others.

Relevant Facts

- Compared to other democracies, the U.S. ranks toward the bottom of the list in the percentage of people who vote (26th out of 32).[67] The reasons why Americans don't vote? Besides apathy, voter turnout in the U.S. is suppressed by several practices and situations:
  - Voter ID laws. People can be prevented from voting because they don't have proper documentation/identification. On its face, this sounds reasonable. But in many instances, it is not easy for people to acquire the documentation required by legislation.
  - Thirty-four states have voter ID laws that require or request voters to present specific forms of ID at the polls.
  - Seven states (Georgia, Indiana, Kansas, Mississippi, Tennessee, Virginia, Wisconsin) have "strict" voter ID requirements – if the ID is not presented at the polls, the person must vote with a provisional ballot and return with the proper ID after the election for it to be counted.[68]

---

[67] Drew Desilver, *Pew Research*, "U.S. trails most developed countries in voter turnout"

[68] Paul Specht, *PolitiFact*, "States with voter ID laws have seen 'zero decrease' in

- Some voter ID laws require a voter to have a government issued ID. But an estimated 11% of Americans do not have one and would have to navigate bureaucratic hurdles to get one.[69]

     These hurdles include:
     - Not being able to get to the offices that provide this service (because of lack of transportation).
     - Not having the documentation needed to receive an ID.
     - Not having the information sometimes required be shown on an ID. For example, North Dakota ID law requires a resident street address, but Native Americans living on reservations don't have a street address.[70]

- Preventing those who've done jail time from voting. The historic trend in the U.S. has been to disenfranchise people who are convicted of crimes, to varying degree state by state.[71] The status quo is now trending towards restoring the rights of these people to vote, but MUCH progress still remains to be made.

---

turnout, NC Republican says"
[69] ACLU, "Fighting Voter ID Requirements"
[70] ACLU, "Voter ID Restrictions Imposed Since 2010"
[71] Sentencing Project, "Issues: Felony Disenfranchisement"

- o Only two states (Maine and Vermont) have no restrictions on the voting rights of felons.
- o Fourteen states and the District of Columbia prevent felons from voting while incarcerated but restore their voting rights once released.
- o Twenty-two states repeal felons' voting rights while imprisoned and afterwards on parole/probation, with voting rights automatically restored after this period – though in some of these states, felons may have to pay any outstanding fines, fees and restitutions before they can vote again.
- o Twelve states indefinitely remove felons' voting rights for some crimes, or require a governor's pardon to have them restored, or mandate an additional waiting period after probation/parole.[72]

- Reducing access to voting places. From 2013 to 2016, at least 868 voting places were closed in Southern states that were previously covered by the Voting Rights Act.[73]

These closures are from only half the counties tracked by the Voting Rights Act for histories of discrimination, so there is every reason to think that there are many more. Fewer polling stations mean longer lines at those that remain, more

---

[72] National Conference of State Legislatures, "Felon Voting Rights"
[73] Matt Vasilogambros, *Pew Trusts*, "Polling Places Remain a Target Ahead of November Elections"

difficulties in getting to them for voters who lost their closest polling place, and disincentives for people to take the time to vote.[74]

- Other inequities diminish the impact of votes that are cast. The way in which the districts are drawn tends to give preferences to certain parties. Therefore, it is very hard for a candidate not a member of that party to get elected in these areas.

- The structure of the U.S. Senate discriminates against an increasing number of American voters. Wyoming, a state with less than one million people, has the same representation as California, which has 30 million.

Yes, the Founding Fathers intended it this way to grant all states equal representation. However, at that time, the states were very, very sensitive to their individual identities and powers. This issue has by and large been resolved in the ensuing 250 years. To have this imbalance in the modern day means that the wishes of millions of Americans are not respected in terms of representation.

Third Force Ideas

---

[74] German Lopez, *Vox*, "7 specific ways states made it harder for Americans to vote in 2016"

Third Force Idea #1: All Americans are REQUIRED to vote. Those who do not will incur some type of penalty or forego a tax credit.

Third Force Idea #2: All Americans must be educated to be intelligent voters and critical thinkers.

Third Force Idea #3: Barriers to keep voters away from the polls or to stop them from voting must be removed. Additionally, we must move toward a secure digital voting system.

Third Force Idea #4: Candidates for national office should be vetted for integrity and conflicts of interest before they are allowed to be on the ballot.

The Obligations

Obligation #1: VOTE.

Obligation #2: Remove the barriers that keep people from voting.

Obligation #3: Get educated about the issues. Understand how this country operates so you can make intelligent decisions.

Obligation #4: Use your intuition and intelligence in making decisions and choosing leaders. If someone does not live by the values they preach, they are not your person. Move on until you find candidates whose integrity matches their rhetoric.

The Roadmap

- Set the intent – What is our vision of how voting rights should be protected and how candidates are truly chosen by popular vote?
- Determine the terminology we can all get behind. "Every American deserves the right to vote and select America's leaders. Voting is a responsibility and an obligation."
- Activate a massive campaign to motivate, educate and enfranchise voters, especially young ones.
- Make election days national holidays for people to vote.
- Develop a hack-proof mechanism for online voting.

Exercise for Chapter 15

What do you think should be done to ensure that all Americans vote?

_____

_____

_____

_____

Chapter 16

The "Fake News" Epidemic, and Its Cure

Did the President have his wife murdered? That's what the tabloid said.

What evidence existed that backed up this "news" story? Well, nothing really. But millions read the headlines during the election season and were influenced in how they viewed the President, and his candidacy.

So, what did the President do? He chose to ignore the damaging fake news story. Instead, he recognized the root of the problem and took action, creating a new position in the Cabinet and a new department in government, The Office of Digital Technology.

Acknowledging that America and Americans faced a huge emerging threat that no one had anticipated, he acted like a leader. He found a solution that rose above his personal trauma and addressed the big picture.

Who was this paragon? His name is Tom Kirkman, and he's the main character in the TV series, "Designated Survivor.:"

Yes, this story is – unfortunately – too good to be true. Would that we could have a real President Kirkman to guide us today.

The Truth About "Fake News"

Here's real news: We have a huge problem with dishonesty in communication that is brainwashing voters, damaging the reputation of innocent people, casting doubt on the integrity and veracity of mainstream media, and convincing millions that lies are facts, with no accountability at all for the perpetrators. Consider these questions:

- Why should lies go unproven and unpunished?
- Why must individuals who are slandered have to hire a lawyer and sue in order to try to get justice?
- Why isn't the burden of proof on those who make these accusations?
- Why do public officials have no accountability to prove what they claim?
- Why isn't lying to the public or in the media, a crime?

The sorry fact is that we've gotten so accustomed to dishonesty, we are numb. Situations that were outrageous in the past, now aren't even publicly noted and commented. It's as if we expect that people do and will lie – public figures, businesspeople, citizens. There is an epidemic of "no fault" betrayals of truth and manipulation.

The Unspoken Consequence

There's another danger in the tolerance for falsehoods. Rumors, conspiracy theories and lies about various groups and individuals fuel violence. Remember the gunman who stormed into the pizza parlor, convinced by social media content that a Presidential candidate was running a child porn ring on the premises? In reality this was a story concocted by a group of teenagers in Greece who wanted to make money by getting people to click through on this outrageous fantasy. Yet, people believed it. That situation could easily have had tragic consequences.

What about the shooters who are goaded by the hatred, bigotry and misogyny found on the dark web and who do commit violence, snuffing out the lives of innocent Americans? When caught, they are prosecuted. But what about the communities and the individuals who preached violence and gave them the ideas to commit these crimes?

People who incite others to violence are supposedly guilty of crimes. Why aren't they prosecuted and – even better – shut down and removed form a position of having an audience?

Even children are subjected to verbal abuse and bullying, often online, that damages them to the point where they may feel that suicide is the only answer. In fact, the rate of suicide is going up. Why is this bullying not a crime?

Other countries who have experienced mass violence have learned the lesson that speech is a weapon.

Two tourists in Germany who gave the Nazi salute in public were arrested under Germany's laws forbidding the display of Nazi symbols or slogans.[75] The falsehoods, over-the-top nationalism, and hatred of minorities expressed by the vicious demagogue Adolph Hitler led to the moral bankruptcy and the physical destruction of their country and their citizens. Subsequent generations reversed course and now Germany is the humanistic and economic leader of Europe.

Do Americans have to experience such suffering to learn the same lesson?

No, we don't, IF we wake up and take bold action based on the realities of today's world.

"Free speech" has traditionally been used to defend lies and hateful rhetoric – but no one has the right to hurt others. Banning speech that incites violence toward others is a no-brainer.

The Positions

Some believe that if a politician is serving their political goals, it's OK to ignore their dishonesty. Or they can rationalize that there are two sides to every story, and the other side is probably lying. They believe stories of how they are persecuted and the victims of conspiracies of all kinds, and only the people in their "bubble" of

---

[75] *BBC*, "Chinese tourists arrested for Hitler salute in Germany"

information are telling them the truth. The Russians didn't really flood social media with propaganda; that information came from their family and people like them.

Others are tempted to ignore falsehoods, particularly the more outrageous ones, rather than spread them further. Taken too far, this means that the truth is never spoken.

People try to be "politically correct" and "play fair" and to give equal time to others, when instead they should be strongly speaking their truth and calling BS on the falsehoods and those who perpetrate them. Taking the moral high ground does not mean maintaining a decorous silence and expecting people to figure it out for themselves. They won't. Truth must be more vocal than untruths.

Relevant Facts

What is the danger of false statements? As cited by Cailin O'Connor and James Weatherall, in "The Misinformation Age: How False Beliefs Spread" (https://amzn.to/2m2jysf),

- Repeated often and loudly, falsehoods start to be accepted as truth. Humans are biased to believe that what is familiar, is true. The more they hear something, the more inclined they are to believe it.
- Taking one fact from a study, and ignoring multiple other contradictory facts, can be used to convince people that the study means something other than

what it actually found or discovered. People hear the one fact, and are influenced to ignore all the other evidence that is contrary to this statement.

- Humans are conformists. They are likely to want to believe what they hear people around them saying. They want to fit in, not stand out in a negative way. Once a group of people start saying the same thing, the chances of individuals in this group of being open to or pursuing another viewpoint goes down considerably.

Until 2011, the FCC's Fairness Doctrine required that television and radio stations with a broadcast license from the FCC dedicate some programming to "controversial issues of public importance", and allow opposing views on those issues to be aired as well.[76] These regulations were in effect to insure that news was balanced, and not just the opinions or propaganda of whoever owned the news medium. These regulations are no longer in place, removing the requirements that media be unbiased.

Most traditional media still abide by these guidelines, even though they are no longer enforceable. However, there's a boomerang effect that is occurring. When legitimate news media present both sides, what if the other side is untruthful? How is that handled? Are they still obligated ethically to report statements that are false or unsubstantiated? Remember that people believe things they hear often.

---

[76] Dylan Matthews, *The Washington Post*, "Everything you need to know about the Fairness Doctrine in one post"

Recently, news media has been more vocal in reporting statements that are not back by evidence, in citing that there is no evidence backing the claim. However, other "news outlets" can influence millions with propaganda with no checks and balances.

The Third Force Ideas

Third Force Idea 1: Set up penalties for lying – for politicians, for disinformation that is spread on social media, for misinformation reported by media. Those who make statements must bear the burden of proof that they are true.

Third Force Idea 2: Develop a rating system for public information – vet it based on its veracity.

Third Force Idea 3: Police social media. Block disinformation and propaganda, and outright falsehoods. If sites and sources persistently tell lies, brand them as such.

Third Force Idea 4: Hold citizens to the same standard of honesty as political officials. People who lie under oath should have criminal charges brought against them. Those who commit fraud – lying to someone who then acts on these lies and is harmed – should be prosecuted as a criminal offense. Crimes committed by misusing powers of attorneys should be just that – crimes.

The Obligations

Obligation #1: Hold everyone – from average Americans to top business tycoons to the nation's leaders – to standards of honesty and personal integrity. Don't slap hands, and don't ignore it. There must be very real penalties for lying if we are going to change behaviors and be able to trust each other again.

Obligation #2: Hold every channel of communication – from social media to digital communications to media organizations to public officials – to this standard. Stop protecting sources of misinformation. Call B.S., call it loudly and publicly, and call it often.

Obligation #3: Victims should not have to bear the cost of getting justice, by having to hire attorneys to get restitution. When faced with the evidence of multiple commission of perjury – lying under oath – a lawyer should not ignore this fact and refuse to bring it up, saying "everyone lies." (True story). Everyone does not lie, and those that do should be called on their behavior and held accountable. The plague of liars screaming their falsehoods so loudly and often that they become accepted as reality, must stop. Call B.S. on this!

The Roadmap

- Set the intention.
- Select the terminology will be acceptable to everyone in talking about this issue: Every

individual and every public entity is accountable for honesty.

- Develop criteria for offenses involving dishonesty for public figures and those being deposed or tried – lying to the public and committing perjury must not be tolerated.
- Develop a way to police digital communications – protecting free speech but identifying sources of communication that are not true.
- Stop the preaching of violence, in any communication channel.

Exercise for Chapter 16

What do you think about the ideas proposed in this chapter to differentiate free speech from damaging falsehoods?

_____

_____

_____

_____

_____

_____

_____

*"The Chinese use two brush strokes to write the word
'crisis'. One brush stroke stands for danger: the other for
opportunity. In a crisis, be aware of the danger – but
recognize the opportunity."*

— *President John F. Kennedy*

Chapter 17 – Third Force Ideas Behind Our Transformation

By now you've read some startling recommendations that
may seem contrary to prevailing opinion on either side of
the political spectrum. This is a good thing. We need new
ideas – more Third Force inspiration – to chart our future
course.

Let's review some of these ideas.

1. In light of modern-day realities, we need to take
    another look at how we define our freedoms. In
    some instances, we have too much freedom and
    too little responsibility.

2. Our understanding of Americans must be informed
    by their biologic reactions to fear and uncertainty. If
    Americans were a "bell curve," we'd see the
    majority in the middle, with one side moving
    toward structure, and the other flexibility in their
    attitudes and their psychology.

3. Everyone living in America has a responsibility to give back to this country. NO ONE gets a free ride. Freedom is not free. In return for living in America and enjoying the benefits in this country, everyone should be prepared to give back – first by voting, second by paying taxes, and third by contributing specifically for benefits they receive.

   For example:

   • By working to maintain good health if they are given health care services.
   • By finding a productive job or participating in a volunteer or work program in return for a free education.
   • By demonstrating good citizenship through fair and just treatment of others.
   • By acts of service to children, to those in need, to neighborhoods, and communities.

4. Rampant capitalism doesn't fit as an economic model for today. Free enterprise yes, innovation yes, but trusting wealthy people to do what is good for the country is not working. Trickle-down economics fueled the concentration of wealth in the hands of a few and is why the average American can't have health care, an affordable college education, or even roads without potholes.

5. The exercise of what one person sees as a right cannot harm others. If someone dies or is harmed,

the individual exercising their rights is responsible for that damage. And it is mandatory to put laws into effect to prevent that harm from happening.

6. Freedom of speech is not freedom to lie. We need new guidelines on what constitutes balanced coverage, a way to identify false information presented as truth, and label it, and to prosecute for perpetration of fraud. Publishing false information should be a criminal, not civil, offense.

7. People running for national government offices should go through a vetting process before being allowed to run, including full disclosure of financial records.

   Since the majority fall in the middle, this is where we must find common ground – where people share commitments to family, integrity, justice, and prosperity. As we move to the ends of the bell curve – and those in the middle may cringe upon reading this – here's where the freedom of belief comes in: freedom to be the person you want to be, as long as no one is hurt by your behavior.

A Ground-Breaking Third Force Idea: One/Thirty

What if every American gave one day a month to his or her country? One day out of thirty in service to others, to help people personally and build a stronger community and country.

There are about 300 million Americans. Many of them are children, the elderly and the disabled who may not be able to make such a contribution. Although, children could work alongside their parents, and those whose mobility is restricted could do projects from home. But let's say, 100 million Americans make this pledge to provide one day a month (or the equivalent), to service of others. That is the equivalent of 5 million people working full time for America and Americans.

That's more than the combined workforce of America's eight largest employers (starting with Walmart which employs 2.2 million people).

That's more than the population of Chicago and Houston combined.

That's more people than live in the state or South Carolina, or the state of Alabama.

Once this idea takes off, schools, churches, and non-profit organizations can organize days and projects for participation.

And what could this inspired and powerful army of volunteers accomplish?

They could:
- Support teachers and students in classrooms
- Visit and support the elderly and disabled

- Participate in projects to help reverse climate change
- Staff help lines
- Harvest unused produce for food banks
- Turn unused land into gardens
- Plant trees
- Mentor foster children and those in need of adult role models
- Volunteer in health care organizations
- Participate in activities to raise money for good causes
- Campaign for causes that will help build a better America
- Teach literacy
- Teach English to new Americans
- Coach sports
- Build housing

The list goes on and on!

Making one/thirty a new American tradition isn't a fantasy. It can happen with the power of intention and cooperation.

Exercise for Chapter 17

You've taken some time to define what you want to see for America. Go back to those written responses and refresh your mind with that vision before starting on the final chapters.

How would you change the vision of America you wrote down, based on your reading of these chapters?

_____

_____

_____

_____

_____

_____

_____

"I believe that people are inherently good."

— Anne Frank

"Some men see things as they are and say, why; I dream things that never were and say, why not."

— Robert F. Kennedy

Chapter 18

The Roadmap to Unity: From You to the Universe

The list of issues and ideas treated in "Magenta Nation" is far from complete.

However, we have a blueprint for change, starting with ourselves and spreading out to our community, the nation and the world. Do not be discouraged by the magnitude of the challenge. Know that miracles do happen. Within a generation, or less, you can help build a new nation and a new society, one that realizes the dream of our forefathers and of Americans today. Every journey starts with that single step.

Let's return to our premise of the power of united intentionality, coupled with the power of service. To help you move forward, here's the step-by-step roadmap for you personally, for your family and community, and for the nation.

It Starts With You – Spirit and Intention

1. What kind of citizen do you want to be? What would you be like if you were your version of the ideal American? Set your intention. Put yourself in spiritual boot camp to make it happen.
2. Find a way each day to consciously and proactively act according to this ideal. Your responsibility, if you do nothing else, is to put positive grains of sand on the scales of justice. Eventually, the positive side weighs more, and goodness wins.
3. Each night, before going to sleep, consciously review your actions and how you expressed this ideal.
4. Find times every day to reflect on your vision of America and to make positive statements about it. These can be prayers if you would like. With this exercise you are doing two things – adding positive intentionality to the world and eliminating negative thoughts that would normally be ruminating in your brain.
5. You CAN find time to create an Intentional America! How? Train your brain when you have downtime to form positive thoughts about the America and the life you would like to see.

Now, before you can finish responding, "*I have no downtime,*" let me say that yes, I know you don't. Very few busy Americans have time to themselves. However, there are many times during the day that our thoughts are free to roam, and we just don't realize these opportunities.

Here's my list of such situations:
- Driving home after dropping the kids of at school/soccer/birthday parties, etc.
- Being on hold on the phone.
- Waiting for elevators.
- Taking a shower and/or personal grooming.
- At the beauty shop or manicurist.
- Waiting for machines to start/work/get fixed.
- In the bathroom.
- Commuting alone.
- Waiting in line for coffee.
- Waiting in line at the drive-through, anything.
- Housecleaning.
- Before falling asleep.
- When worrying – replace those fearful thoughts with positive ones!

When you find yourself in one of these situations, remind yourself that this is an opportunity to visualize and pray for America and the life you want.

Mind is the Builder

Work with the section on Third Force Ideas and select the ones you think are most promising. Select three to investigate further, and maybe make them your cause. Write here the Third Force Ideas you like best:

1.

2.

3.

Transforming Our Communities

1. Practice the techniques in Chapter 3 when talk turns negative around politics or society. This may take some effort. It's important not to participate in negative, malicious, or cruel put-downs.

    A good way to respond is to say, "What's really important here is…" and bring the conversation around to the issue. Encourage discussion about positive solutions. Learn dialogue terms and techniques that bring agreement, not divisiveness.

2. Volunteer. Yes, we know you have no time. If you have children, you're probably already engulfed in volunteerism at their school. If you are a member of a church, you probably volunteer there. You may already have your favorite causes to which you give your time and resources.

    But if you are not doing something to give to others, START. It may be just:
    - Listening to older people who are lonely
    - Donating your old clothes to a cause
    - Adding more to a collection box or sharing positive thoughts and stories you find on the Internet to give others a lift.

Find a way to give to your community and to others in need. These connections nurture compassion in you as well as help others.

3. And especially, make the effort to help children or one child. Taking an interest in them, helping at school, clubs, scouts, orphanages, foster care. Children desperately need adults who care about them. And NEVER tolerate the physical or emotional abuse of a child. Never.

4. If you can, involve your family and friends in these efforts. For many years my husband and I sponsored children from around the world. When we had children, they became part of that tradition. We wrote letters together and picked out holiday presents together.

   Our kids learned about these children and their lives and a very different set of circumstances for growing up. They saw how their efforts made a real difference in helping these young people be fed, clothed, educated, and inspired. And they made friends around the world.

The Physical is the Result

With intentions set and creative ideas in mind, we move into action. We start by building a strong community: the communities in which we live, including our families, are the next focus of our national renaissance.

Transforming Our Families and Communities:

1. Find ways for your family to share a few minutes of positive thought, gratitude or prayer, each day. Get family members involved in sharing their ideas and feelings. If your family will cooperate, you can go through the exercises in Chapter 1 with them!

2. Each day, do something positive for each person in your life – your family members, co-workers, friends you see. Even if it is just a big smile and a genuine *"How are you?"* you will be amazed at how popular you become, and the impact that you have.

Revive the Nation

1. PRAY/SET YOUR INTENTION. The power of a positive intention doesn't just change us, it changes the world. It changes our reality.

2. LEARN. Get informed about our country. In past years we've learned how much misinformation there is about everything from politicians to world events. This is a major challenge to our country and the world right now.

   With all the new channels of information we have, how do we know what is true? Still, make the effort to be informed. Don't just stick to what is going on in your neighborhood or your group of like-minded people. Watch and read what others think as well. Don't live in a bubble!

3. VOTE. The U.S. has one of the lowest records for voter turnout of any developed nation. Every American needs to understand the issues and vote. It is the most important action we can take for our country. Be sure the candidates and causes you support are in line with your values! If someone doesn't live their espoused values, they are not your person.

4. SERVE. Get involved in at least one cause that impacts the future of our country. Read about it, think about it, form an opinion and take action to communicate that opinion.

    Here are just a few ideas:
    -   Addiction
    -   Availability for healthcare
    -   Availability of jobs
    -   Bullying
    -   Care for the elderly
    -   Clean energy
    -   Education
    -   Food availability and safety
    -   Housing
    -   Justice for minorities
    -   Literacy
    -   Rehabilitation in prisons
    -   Voter registration

- Waste disposal

At some point, you may want to move towards a leadership position to better impact our country and our world. It might be running for the school board, a local office, a position in a union, or a state or national office. Or, it could be a volunteer position helping to elect a candidate. This is the highest form of service to your country! Go for it!

5. <u>And finally, very important: STOP JUDGING, start listening.</u> Be patient, with yourself and with others. Change takes time and miracles can happen in an instant.

The "Quick Reference" Guide to Change

For those of you who prefer a condensed version of the guide for change, here are the seven steps to transforming America:

1. <u>Find your spiritual center.</u> Accept that "it starts with me." Aspire to be the ideal citizen in your vision of America. Then, set your intention for America.
2. <u>Keep the vision</u> of your ideal America in your mind and heart. Harness the power of intentionality. Visualize it, imagine it, see it as real.
3. <u>Stop judging. Start listening</u> and hearing the other person's point of view. Think of the Third Force Ideas you believe can be solutions and talk about them to build bridges.

4. <u>Start helping.</u> Service is the way out of today's dilemmas.
5. <u>Learn dialogue and terminology</u> that bring discussions to agreement, not divisiveness.
6. <u>Act</u> to make your vision, reality.

Thank you for reading this book. Before you set it aside or delete it from your Kindle (or better yet, pass it on to someone else), please pause for one moment and bring to mind, one more time, your vision for this wonderful country. If you do nothing else, keep the vision in your consciousness. Return to it when you are stressed or discouraged. Make a focused effort to think about this idea every day. Nothing can stop the power of a good idea.

Remember the stirring words of Winston Churchill, spoken when Great Britain stood alone against destruction by the world's most evil regime:

> *"We shall not flag or fail. We shall go on to the end... We shall fight on the beaches, we shall fight on the landing grounds, we shall fight in the fields and in the streets, we shall fight in the hills; we shall never surrender..."*

And remember also these words of wisdom:

> *"All this will not be finished in the first one hundred days. Nor will it be finished in the first one thousand days, nor in the lifetime of this administration, nor even*

perhaps in our lifetime on this planet. But let us begin."
– John F. Kennedy

To victory and a new nation!

Made in the USA
San Bernardino, CA
15 June 2020

73498286R00095